PUFFIN BOOKS

FIRST TERM AT TREBIZON

Lonely and afraid, Rebecca Mason's journey from London to the west country to begin her first term at Trebizon, one of England's most famous girls' boarding schools, gets off to a miserable start. Tearfully waving goodbye to her parents, who are going to live in Saudi Arabia, she is coldly and abruptly told to stop leaning out of the train by a prefect, Elizabeth Exton, editor of the school's magazine *The Trebizon Journal* and daughter of a well-known business tycoon.

But arriving at the school Rebecca is at once captivated by Trebizon Bay which the school overlooks, and at the first opportunity escapes to the beach for a few minutes on her own. There she puts her thoughts and first impressions into writing – a poem. Discarded and quickly forgotten, Rebecca little realizes that the poem will bring her into dramatic conflict with Elizabeth Exton.

Caught up in the whirl of school life, Rebecca has little time to feel homesick despite her initial fears. Soon she is firm friends with Tish Anderson and Sue Murdoch, despite Debbie Rickard's attempts to prevent it. And her hopes of making her mark on the school in her first term seem set to be fulfilled when an essay she writes is accepted for inclusion in the jubilee edition of *The Trebizon Journal* – that is, until the magazine is published!

Widely acclaimed, this modern boarding school story is the first of an immensely popular series.

Anne Digby was born in Kingston upon Thames, Surrey but has lived in the west country for many years. As well as the Trebizon books she is the author of the popular *Me, Jill Robinson* stories.

THE TREBIZON BOOKS (in reading order)

ANNE DIGBY

FIRST TERM AT
TREBIZON

PUFFIN BOOKS

PUFFIN BOOKS

Published by the Penguin Group
27 Wrights Lane, London w8 5TZ, England
Viking Penguin Inc., 40 West 23rd Street, New York, New York 10010, USA
Penguin Books Australia Ltd, Ringwood, Victoria, Australia
Penguin Books Canada Ltd, 2801 John Street, Markham, Ontario, Canada L3R 1B4
Penguin Books (NZ) Ltd, 182–190 Wairau Road, Auckland 10, New Zealand

Penguin Books Ltd, Registered Offices: Harmondsworth, Middlesex, England

First published by W. H. Allen 1978
Published in Puffin Books 1988

Made and printed in Great Britain by
Cox & Wyman Ltd, Reading
Filmset in Linotron Ehrhardt by
Rowland Phototypesetting Ltd, Bury St Edmunds, Suffolk

CONTENTS

ONE

GOING AWAY TO SCHOOL

'Have a good first term, Rebecca. Try and be happy.'

'Remember, this is a wonderful chance for you. And you'll soon make new friends.'

'Yes, Mum. Yes, Dad.'

Rebecca's voice was flat. It was a Tuesday morning. Her trunk had been loaded into the luggage van. Her hand luggage was up on the rack in an empty compartment somewhere down the corridor. She had deliberately dodged the carriage reserved for new girls.

Now she was in the corridor of the train, leaning out of the window while her parents, on the platform below, kissed her goodbye.

'Off you go!'

They stepped back as the train started to move away. What a forlorn little figure their daughter looked, half-drowned in her brand new school cape, an arm reaching out of it to wave. The breeze was wrapping her fair hair round her face.

Rebecca thought how grand some of the people on the platform looked, seeing their daughters off on the train, and how small and round and homely her own parents looked in comparison.

'I hope you like it out there –' she called, her voice hoarse. She pushed her hair out of her eyes with the back of her hand, brushing away a tear at the same time.

'We'll be back in England for Christmas,' called her mother. 'We'll all be together again. Write to us!'

'And write something for that school magazine!' shouted her father.

Rebecca waved as hard as she could; the platform seemed to be sliding rapidly backwards, her parents getting smaller and smaller. It was as though all her past life were slipping away, a dreadful feeling.

'Get your head in!'

Rebecca did not hear, but just kept on waving. By leaning out as far as she could, she could still see them – little pin people – way back there on the platform. They were going, going . . . gone.

'Are you deaf?'

Somebody grabbed the back of her dark blue cape and pulled her in and then, getting their fingertips under the top metal edge of the window, slid it up and snapped it shut.

'Can't you read? You're not supposed to lean out of the window,' said the voice.

Her eyes blurred, Rebecca could not see the person properly, except that she was a girl in a checked coat. As far as Rebecca could tell she had nothing to do with either British Rail or Trebizon School. She had her back to her now as she bent down to pick up a large black bag that she had dumped down in the corridor of the train.

'Mind your own business!' said Rebecca, angry and miserable.

The girl stood up, holding the bag, and turned round to

face Rebecca. Her brown eyes had narrowed down to frightening slits. Her whole appearance was striking, indeed, overpowering. She had long black wavy hair, bony features and a rather hawk-like nose. She towered above Rebecca for she was almost grown-up and very tall and elegant. She wore her beautifully cut tweed coat open and with graceful flair. Under the coat she was wearing a blue skirt, cream blouse and striped tie, and a navy v-necked jumper. This was the winter uniform of Trebizon School, the same outfit that Rebecca herself was wearing. Sixth Formers could wear a winter coat of their own choice in place of the regulation blue cape, and this girl was a Sixth Former.

'Did you say something to me?'

Rebecca hung her head, cheeks hot with embarrassment. She felt very small and insignificant in front of this imposing figure.

'I was rude. I'm sorry.'

'What's your name?'

'Rebecca Mason.'

'Ever been away to school before?'

'No.'

'Heard of prefects?'

Rebecca's spirit sank even further.

'I'm both a prefect and school officer, if that means anything to you. My name is Elizabeth Exton. If you don't mind me saying so, you'd better learn a few manners if you want to fit in at Trebizon.'

'Elizabeth!' shouted a girl from the other end of the corridor. She, too, was tall and grown-up looking and was wearing a camel-hair coat over her school uniform. 'Come on! I've found a free table in the Buffet Car!'

Elizabeth Exton crooked her arm round the bulging black

bag, rather like a doctor's, and hugged it close to her as though its contents were very important.

'Okay, Emma. Coming!'

She moved off along the swaying corridor without looking back.

Rebecca wondered where she had heard the name Exton before, and what was in the black bag, and just what was meant by a 'school officer'. But she didn't really care. She turned and pressed her forehead against the cool glass of the corridor window and watched the railway sidings slipping past.

It seemed a bad omen, somehow, getting on the wrong side of a prefect the minute she had set foot on the train. So she would have to learn some manners if she wanted to fit in, would she? 'Rotten boarding school!' she thought savagely. She had no desire to go to Saudi Arabia with her parents, now that her father had been posted there by his firm. She knew that was impossible, anyway. But if only she could have stayed in London, at her day school, with all her friends!

'As the firm is paying, we may as well have the best,' Mr Mason had told his wife, trying to sound nonchalant, although in reality he was still rather stunned by the news of his promotion, and the fact that full boarding school fees for his daughter went with it. He had been to a very ordinary school himself. 'Trebizon is the one with the big reputation. They turn out musicians, artists, novelists – all sorts. If they've got any talent a place like that brings it out.'

'We could never afford it ourselves,' agreed Mrs Mason, though not without a pang. 'It's on the coast, too. It's the chance of a lifetime for Rebecca, and I'm sure she'll make the most of it.'

It was true that Rebecca wanted to be a writer when she grew up, and she had already won prizes in poem and essay competitions. It was also true that her new school produced a magazine each term, *The Trebizon Journal*, that was quite breathtaking to look at – a copy had been sent to her parents with the school prospectus. Not only was it thick and glossy, like a real magazine, but it had some really good stuff in it, and all the writing and art work was done by girls at the school.

'See what it says here,' her father had said, holding up the Principal's Summer Newsletter, which had been tucked in a pocket at the back of the prospectus with a lot of other bits and pieces. He quoted from the Newsletter: 'It has long been a tradition at Trebizon that the girls who rise to the position of Editor of our own *Trebizon Journal* seem to go forward to carve out for themselves a distinguished career. We are sure that the past year's Editor, Mary Green, who has been offered a post on a national newspaper, will prove no exception to this rule.'

Standing in the train's corridor, it suddenly came to Rebecca where she had heard the name Exton before. Wasn't Fred Exton a well-known business tycoon, always 'taking over' small companies? Hadn't there been something about him, in the same Newsletter, in connection with the school magazine?

'Until recently, it looked as though increases in printing and paper costs would force us to publish *The Trebizon Journal* once a year in future, instead of once a term. Thanks to the generosity of a parent, Mr Fred Exton, to whom we owe a deep debt of gratitude, the magazine is to continue on its present termly basis and a tradition that goes back fifty years thus remains unbroken.'

Rebecca remembered her father giving a chuckle.

'Freddie Exton, eh? Glad to see he's been putting his ill-gotten gains to some useful purpose.' Later, taking his

11

daughter's hand, he had said, 'Who knows, Becky? You might become the Editor of that magazine yourself, one of these days.'

Yet none of this could make Rebecca feel enthusiastic about coming to Trebizon. As she watched the factories and housing estates of west London racing past, sombre on the grey September morning, she felt only the dull ache of homesickness.

Suddenly she heard laughter. Two girls came rushing into the corridor from the next carriage, laden with hand luggage, their blue capes flapping. They looked about Rebecca's age.

'Shove over!' said the first one, a girl with jet black curly hair, turned up nose and an enormous laughing mouth.

Rebecca shrank against the window, her back firmly turned, as first the dark girl and then her friend, who had sandy-coloured shoulder-length hair and spectacles, squeezed past her.

'Thanks!'

'Let's find a compartment, Tish,' said the sandy-haired one. 'We've shaken her off.'

'I suppose even Roberta Jones can take a hint.'

With much giggling and scuffling of feet they made their way along the corridor, peering into compartments as they went.

'I could have screamed when she walked in!' Rebecca heard the dark-haired girl called Tish say. 'Imagine having to listen to *her* voice all the way!'

'Look!' There was a whoop of joy. 'An empty one!'

The door of a compartment slid to and Rebecca sighed. The corridor was silent again now; just the sound of the train rushing over the rails. Seeing those two, obviously close, reminded her of another dreadful fact. She was being pitched into Trebizon in the Second Year. Everyone else would have been there a whole year; they would all be fixed up with friends, in twosomes and threesomes, like her and Claire and Amanda, the two friends she had left behind in London.

Rebecca felt weary. She must find her compartment, sit down, read a book or something – anything to take her mind off things. She walked down the corridor, trying to remember where she had left her hand luggage. The first three compartments were all occupied – it must have been about the fourth one along where she had left her things.

She peered into it and found herself staring directly in at the two girls who had passed her just now. They had taken over the entire compartment, sprawled out on the seats, amongst a scattering of belongings: hockey sticks, a violin case, and carrier bags that spilled out sweets, books and oranges. The black-haired girl looked up and saw her and seemed to scowl.

Her cheeks hot, Rebecca quickly turned on her heel and hurried back along the corridor the way she had come. She stood once more by the window and stared out, feeling confused. Had those two taken over her compartment? It looked like it.

'Hey!' The black-haired one had slid back the glass door and stuck out her head, calling to Rebecca. 'Thought you were somebody else. Are you lost? There's a denim bag and a hockey stick in here, up on the rack.'

Slowly, Rebecca retraced her steps and entered the compartment. She looked up and saw her bag and then sat down in the corner by the door and took a paperback book out of the deep pocket inside her cape.

'You're new aren't you? First or Second Year?'

'Second.'

'Like us. You'll be in Juniper then. I'm Ishbel Anderson. Tish for short, and this is Sue Murdoch.'

'Hallo,' said Rebecca politely, then opened her book and started to read.

'Do you have a name?' The huge grin came again. 'Or did your parents forget to give you one?'

'Rebecca Mason,' she replied, without even glancing up from her book.

ALL ABOUT THE MAGAZINE

Rebecca read her book with cool concentration. If these two thought that they had to make conversation with a new girl, just when they had escaped from this Roberta Jones person, they could think otherwise. She could look after herself perfectly well!

After one or two curious glances in her direction, the two friends settled down soon enough to a long, low buzz of conversation that seemed, to Rebecca, all set to last for hours.

'Hallo! Rebecca Mason? I've been looking for you!'

Sliding back the door, a woman put her head into the compartment. She wore chunky jewellery and a thick blue jumper with a high neck and a light grey coat; her hair was blonde, streaked with grey, and swept back off her face and she had clear blue eyes and a friendly smile.

'For me?' asked Rebecca guiltily, looking up from her book.

'Yes, I'm Miss Morgan, your House Mistress. That means –' her nose screwed up as she laughed, 'that I'm supposed to be looking after you on the train. We've got a special carriage for new girls – which makes it sound as though they're infectious, doesn't it? – so they can begin to get to know one another before they get to Trebizon. But you've managed to avoid us nicely!'

'I – I'm sorry,' began Rebecca. She rather liked this person. 'I did see them, but they seemed younger than me, and I thought –'

'Quite right, they are younger. All First Years. And you're going to be a Second Year, aren't you? Like Ishbel and Susan here. As a matter of fact you'll be in the same form as them, too, you're down for II Alpha. And naturally you'll be in Juniper together.'

Juniper House, by far the largest boarding house at Trebizon, was where all girls lived for their first two years there. Miss Morgan came further into the compartment, gripped the luggage rack to steady herself, and raised her voice above the noise of the swaying train as it rushed into a tunnel.

'This is very suitable. Ishbel, Susan, please look after Rebecca for the rest of the journey. Her parents are going to live in Saudi Arabia and she's never been to boarding school before. Rebecca – you'll be comfortable here, so I won't ask you to move.'

She went out into the corridor, leaving an awkward silence.

Rebecca couldn't stand it. She stood up and put her book in her pocket and felt for her money. It made her feel uneasy that Miss Morgan had told these two something about her. She would go for a walk down the train.

'Going somewhere?' asked Tish.

'Just to get a coffee in the Buffet Car,' replied Rebecca.

'D'you want us to come with you?' asked Sue.

'I know I've never been to boarding school before,' said

Rebecca lightly, 'but I think I can find my way around a train.'

The Buffet Car was very nearly full. As Rebecca made her way down the central gangway, looking for an empty seat, she passed two senior Trebizon girls in navy jumpers and blue skirts, with a table to themselves. She recognized the prefect, Elizabeth Exton, and the girl called Emma. They had taken their coats off now and put them up on the rack.

They seemed settled there for the journey. The big black bag was open and up on the table. The two girls' heads were bent close together over some pictures that Elizabeth had spread out on the table. Although Elizabeth was shielding them, rather possessively, Rebecca caught a glimpse of some exquisite line drawings of birds, on artists' pasteboard, beautifully coloured in.

'Elizabeth, some of this stuff's sensational,' she heard Emma say. 'You've been really busy in the holidays.'

'I've met some super people, I can tell you.'

Rebecca found a seat, opposite an elderly gentleman, and ordered a coffee from a steward in a white coat. The coffee arrived in a white carton, with a lid, the cream in a miniature carton beside it; sugar lumps were in a bowl on the table, each lump separately wrapped.

The coffee tasted delicious. Looking out of the window, Rebecca saw rolling green fields, some houses and a church spire. They had left London behind and every minute took the high-speed train further west, towards Trebizon School and her new life.

'Elizabeth Exton must be an artist,' thought Rebecca. No wonder the prefect and her black bag appeared inseparable; it must contain all her holiday work. Was she specializing in Art perhaps, and hoping to go on to one of the big Art

Colleges? The thought that she could produce work like that made her seem an even more imposing and elevated person.

But before long, Rebecca fell to thinking of home, the town house in London where she had been born and brought up, and the sunny little bedroom with all her things in it. It would be strange sleeping in a dormitory with a lot of other girls and she shivered to think of her home, let out to strangers for many months of the year.

'Cheer up,' said the elderly gentleman. 'It won't be as bad as you think. My wife was an old Trebizonian, had the time of her life there. I expect you will, once you settle in.'

'Do I look new, then?' asked Rebecca in surprise.

'Brand new,' he replied, with a smile. 'So does the uniform.'

Rebecca made her way back down the train, feeling slightly more cheerful. For a few moments she had been made to feel as though she had joined a rather nice club, and one that had been going for a long time.

The door of her compartment was open and there was a large girl in there, standing over the other two, hanging on to the luggage rack with one hand and waving some sheets of paper in the other. The girl had brown plaits and a red, rather boyish face, and she was wearing the school uniform, without a cape.

'Honestly, Tish, I'm not asking you to read them this very minute – just put them in your bag –'

Rebecca decided to take her cape off, too. She rolled it up and climbed up on to the seat to put it on the luggage rack, at the same time taking a good squint at the top sheet of paper.

'My Dog' – *a poem by Roberta Jones* it said at the top.

'For the last time, Robert,' Tish said wearily, 'there is no point in putting them in my bag, as I haven't the slightest intention of reading them –'

'Daddy says they're the best poems I've ever written –'

'That's not saying much!' observed Sue Murdoch.

'And they *deserve* to go in the school magazine,' carried on Roberta, who really seemed to have a thick skin. 'In fact, he says they're a lot better than some of the things he's seen in the *Journal*.'

Rebecca settled back in her seat, rather enjoying this. So this was the Roberta Jones they had been trying to escape from! She could see their point of view.

'Look, Robert, I'll be holding a magazine meeting in the next couple of days and calling in all contributions. I'll read the poems then, along with the other stuff people have done in the holidays, and if we all agree with Daddy, they'll be chosen.'

'Of course, if we don't agree with Daddy,' said Sue, 'they won't.' So saying, she got up and took Roberta's elbow and pointedly escorted her out into the corridor.

'You'd better go – we're looking after a new girl – think she's got a headache,' she whispered loudly, and gave the big girl a push. ''Bye!' Then she slid the door firmly shut and threw herself down on her seat and laughed, looking across at Rebecca. 'Hope you didn't mind my saying that!'

'No,' replied Rebecca. But she was staring at Tish, almost eaten up with curiosity. She had hardly been able to believe her ears.

'Are *you* the Editor of *The Trebizon Journal*?' she asked.

The huge grin that was never long absent from Tish's face came back. She and Sue moved along to be opposite Rebecca.

'Good heavens, no!'

'Tish is the Magazine Officer for Juniper,' explained Sue. 'Mainly because she's good at English and very fair and nobody argues with her. It's like being an editor, only on a minor scale. At the start of term, she takes in all the contributions from the House and sifts through them, and asks people's opinions. Then there's another meeting and the best ones are passed round and we all vote –'

'And then two or three are chosen,' explained Tish, 'and the best of the lot has a gold star put on it, which means it's bound to go into the *Journal*. All the Houses do the same. It saves the Editor a lot of work, and makes it all democratic as well.'

'Who is the Editor?' asked Rebecca.

'A girl called Elizabeth Exton, way off in Upper Sixth.'

'Elizabeth –' exclaimed Rebecca. 'But her father –'

There was a moment's silence then, and the two friends looked at one another. They seemed almost embarrassed.

'You know about that then?'

'Well, yes. There was something about it in the Newsletter that was sent to us, with the school prospectus and all that stuff.'

'We think it looks pretty bad,' said Tish. 'And it's almost as bad as it looks! It wasn't that Freddie Exton attached any conditions when he offered to bale out the magazine. It's just that the cheque came through at the end of last term, just before the girls who were going to be in the Upper Sixth this year held their meeting to elect the new Editor.'

'They all knew how much Elizabeth wanted it,' said Sue, carrying on the story, 'and they just voted her in. They probably felt they couldn't do anything else. After all, without her father, there wouldn't be a *Journal* any more, or not as we know it, and now it can carry on for years.'

'But some of us thought she should have declined, all the same,' said Tish. 'Audrey Maxwell would make a much better Editor.'

'It was a proper election, though,' said Sue, 'and they

didn't *have* to vote for her. They must think she'll be pretty good.'

'She'd better be. It's the Golden Jubilee this term – a special issue. A lot of people will be looking at it.'

Rebecca now realized the full significance of Elizabeth Exton's big black bag. She realized she wasn't an artist, after all.

'I've met her,' she said. 'I think she's been working on it all over the holidays. I saw her down in the Buffet Car. She was showing someone some work, some beautiful drawings.'

'She must be keen,' frowned Tish, slightly perplexed, 'if she's been meeting some of the Seniors in the holidays and getting things together even before term starts. It goes to press early in the term, but the Editor doesn't usually collect stuff in till we all get back to school, the way I said.'

'I heard her say she'd met some super people.'

'I expect she has.' Tish wrinkled up her nose, unable to see any significance in that. 'She met the Queen once.'

They fell silent. Rebecca realized that, briefly, she had dropped her defences and had quite enjoyed talking to these two.

'Nice to talk to you,' said Tish then, as though reading her thoughts. 'You're the dead opposite of Roberta Jones and one or two others, who are so full of themselves they can never stop talking.'

'She seems to like herself,' murmured Rebecca.

'I suppose somebody has to,' laughed Tish, and added shrewdly, 'Do you do any writing yourself, poems or anything?'

Rebecca went pink to the roots of her fair hair. 'Of course not,' she said quickly. 'Not really. I just like reading, that's all.'

She got up and got her cape down and found her paperback in the pocket. She felt like being quiet now and settled down with her book while the others returned to their seats and began to chat.

Ishbel Anderson was quite a character, Rebecca decided, and she liked her. But she wanted to get to Trebizon now, and get it over with.

THREE

REBECCA'S POEM

The train pulled in to Trebizon Station at three o'clock in the afternoon. All the girls coming to school on the train from London had eaten a good lunch, some in relays in the Buffet Car and others, like Rebecca, a packed lunch. Now they spilled out on the platform in a crisp display of dark jumpers and blue skirts as porters unloaded dozens of suitcases and trunks from the luggage van on to station trolleys.

'Stick with us,' said Tish, steering Rebecca along the crowded platform. She and Sue were laden with their disorganized mess of carrier bags and hockey sticks and the violin case. Rebecca wore her denim bag slung over her shoulder and clutched her hockey stick and rolled up cape.

The dull September morning in London had turned into a warm, sunny afternoon here in the west country.

'Are you all right?' asked Miss Morgan, looking like a shepherd with the flock of First Years around her, as Rebecca went by. Rebecca nodded.

'Fill the front coach up first!' someone shouted.

'Let's try and grab a front seat,' said Tish, 'then you can get a really good view. Ever seen the place?'

'No, only pictures.'

To make room, the younger girls had to sit three to a seat and Rebecca rather liked being sandwiched between Tish and Sue in the first seat, right by the door. Tish seemed to be very popular.

'Hi, Tish!'

'Where were you on the train?'

'You promised to send me a card from France, you rotten thing!'

'Who's your friend?' asked a plump girl.

'Rebecca Mason,' Tish replied to this question. 'She's going to be in II Alpha with us. Rebecca – this is Sally Elphinstone.'

'Hallo,' said Rebecca shyly. She somehow felt that nothing was too bad while Tish was looking after her. It was a warm, secure feeling – while it lasted.

'Hi! Otherwise known as Elf,' giggled the girl Sally. 'And this is Margot. Margot Lawrence.'

A black girl. Nice. Fun-looking. Probably Elf's best friend. Rebecca dimly remembered seeing them together on the train.

'She'll be in our dormy, too, won't she Tish?' said the black girl. 'Wasn't there something about us getting some-one new in Second Year?'

'You're right, Margot,' said Tish in a matter-of-fact way. 'Hear that, Rebecca?'

'Mmmm,' replied Rebecca, trying not to look pleased or pathetic.

All the luggage loaded on, the double doors shut, the coach climbed steeply up the main street of the old stone-built town of Trebizon, with two more coaches behind. The

24

sun slanted along the pavements and Rebecca noticed children with buckets and spades. This was the tag end of the holiday season and there were several beaches close to the town.

At the top of the town the coach turned left, down a winding road lined with small hotels, most of them set well back in gardens. At the edge of the road there were rhododendron bushes and, every so often, a small palm tree. The coach turned again, out into open country, and there –

'Trebizon Bay!' exclaimed Rebecca. 'Is that it?'

'Yes, that's it. Not bad, is it?'

Through the front window of the coach, Rebecca could see directly down across the fields to a huge bay, fringed with golden sand, the blue sea sparkling and dancing in the sunshine. Not bad? It was beautiful.

'And there's the school,' said Sue, pointing.

Rebecca glimpsed a mixture of white stone buildings and red brick, in amongst tall trees, set in many acres of parkland that ran down to the coast on the west side of Trebizon Bay. In the heart of the cluster of buildings, rising even above the trees, there was a tall tower with a clock, its hands caught brightly in the sun.

Shortly afterwards, the coach turned in through wrought iron entrance gates. White lettering on a large blue board beside the entrance said: TREBIZON SCHOOL. Another sign said: SPEED LIMIT 10 M.P.H. The drive was half a mile long and several times the convoy of coaches had to pull into the side, trees and bushes whispering against the windows, to let cars past, coming from the direction of the school.

'Chaos!' said Tish. 'It's always like this on the first day.'

The coach pulled up in front of the school's main building, a magnificent stone manor house of fine proportions, built for a local nobleman in the eighteenth century. It had a sweeping, gravelled forecourt so large that there was ample room for all.

The girls poured out of the coaches, milling around the parked cars and greeting friends who had been brought to school by road.

'Where are the coaches going off to now?' asked Rebecca.

'Round the back to unload all the luggage,' said Tish, but she was staring at a red mini that was pulling up nearby. Someone in it was waving to her. 'The school staff sort out all the trunks and cases and get them round to the various Houses. It's quite an operation, but with a bit of luck they all get to the right places in time for us to unpack before we have tea.'

'Tish!' cried a joyful voice.

A girl tumbled out of the red mini, parked incongruously beside a huge Rolls-Royce, and came rushing over. She had long black hair tied back, brown eyes and a very tanned skin. She flung her arms round Tish.

'Mara!' said Tish. 'How was Athens? Mara – this is Rebecca Mason, she's going to be in our Year. Rebecca – Mara Leonodis.'

'Hallo.'

'Hallo, Rebecca!' But the girl, who was Greek, had eyes only for Ishbel Anderson and Susan Murdoch. 'Tish – Sue – I've got it! I've got the machine!'

The other two shrieked and dropped their things on to the gravel.

'You haven't!'

'I promised, yes? Come quickly and see, it's in the boot. Soon Anestis will carry it in for us –'

All three of them rushed to the small red car, leaving Rebecca standing there wondering what the excitement was about. Suddenly, dwarfed in the shadow of the big school, of which she had only seen a small part so far, she felt lonely and frightened.

'Rebecca?'

Miss Morgan came striding over, followed by her large party of younger girls. They were lined up in pairs, carrying their hand luggage and their brand new hockey sticks, their blue capes folded over their arms.

'Walk with me,' the Junior House Mistress said kindly. 'I'm taking all you new girls to Juniper. Matron and her staff are waiting to meet you all, and they'll show you what's what.'

Rebecca fell into step beside Miss Morgan. Going up a long, low flight of stone steps to the main doors of the school, she glanced back and saw that the others were still by the red car, crowding round a large cardboard carton that stood on the ground. They had forgotten all about her.

'We'll cut through the old school,' said Miss Morgan, pushing back the large doors; and they all trooped into a magnificent entrance hall.

Coming into the cool building out of the sunshine, Rebecca shivered. The floor was of polished wood and the high ceilings were ornately moulded. The staircase was very grand, with oil-painted murals by an eighteenth-century artist rising up the side. She felt overwhelmed. Just because Tish and Sue had been nice to her – it didn't mean a thing. She was new and she had no friends and now she was actually here, it was terrifying.

Miss Morgan led them along a corridor and then out through a small glass door at the back of the building.

'These are the quadrangle gardens, and that's Juniper House opposite, where you are all going to be living from now on.'

'Going to be living,' thought Rebecca. She felt trapped.

They were in big square gardens, laid to lawn, but criss-crossed with flagstoned paths and dotted with flower beds. There were buildings all around the square: the main house, from which they had emerged, then to one side a converted stable block with the tall clock tower, added as a folly in Victorian times; to the other side a modern block in white stone which housed the school dining and assembly halls, with art rooms and science laboratories on the upper floors.

And directly opposite them, across the gardens forming the fourth side of the square, was Juniper House. It was a perfectly pleasant modern red brick building, that blended in well with the others, but to Rebecca's eyes it suddenly looked like a prison.

They crossed the gardens and entered Juniper House through open french doors at the far end of a long terrace. Matron and Miss Morgan took the main party up the east staircase to the First Year dormitories. They were beginning to chatter excitedly. Rebecca found herself abandoned to Mary, a young Assistant Matron, who took her the entire length of the ground floor and then up the west staircase.

'You're the only new Second Year,' said Mary. 'First, I'll show you your dormitory. You're in number six.'

Number six turned out to be a big room on the second floor, with primrose walls and big windows that faced due south, so that the sun dappled the counterpanes on the beds. There were eight beds in all, spaced well apart, in separate cubicles; each cubicle had its own chest of drawers, bedside locker and small hanging cupboard.

'You're here in the corner,' said Mary.

Rebecca put her bag and cape and hockey stick down on top of her chest of drawers, which was a pale pink. Although her bed was right underneath a large window, she still had the strange sensation of walls closing in on her.

'Have a wash, if you like,' said Mary. 'There'll be other girls coming up in a minute. You can meet them, then – if you like – I'll show you around Juniper, so you know the layout. Your trunk will be up here in about half an hour and you'll have plenty of time to unpack before tea.'

Rebecca's mind took little of this in. A strange whispering sound beyond the open window had caught her attention. She crossed to the window and looked out. What was it she could hear, coming from somewhere beyond those trees?

'Trebizon Bay!' she thought, catching a glimpse of sand and blue sea between the trees. The sound she could hear was the breaking of waves on the sea shore, for the back of Juniper House was less than two hundred yards from the most westerly corner of that huge, beautiful bay she had seen from the coach.

At the same time she heard voices: girls coming up west staircase.

'Please – may I just run down and look at the sea?'

The surprised look on Mary's face made Rebecca realize that she had betrayed something of her desperate impulse to escape.

'What I mean is,' said Rebecca, more calmly, 'I'm dying to stretch my legs after being cooped up in that train for hours.'

'Of course,' Mary nodded. In fact she had a lot of work to do. 'And the bay's lovely. Off you go then. Come back in half an hour, so you can unpack your trunk before tea.'

'Thanks!'

Rebecca snatched up her denim bag and flew out of the door at this end of the dormitory, just as she heard a clamour of voices outside the door at the opposite end. Dodged them! She couldn't bear the thought of being surrounded by them all, looking at her, asking questions. That could come later.

She came down the back stairs and let herself out of a back door. A coach was just turning out of the yard and some men were sorting through a stack of suitcases and trunks, all clearly labelled, and loading them on two land-rovers. Rebecca slipped past them and along a path that led downhill through the trees. There was the sea, beckoning her on.

She emerged from the trees and realized that she was fenced in from the sand dunes beyond by iron palings. Then she saw a small gate, open, with a sign on it: TREBIZON SCHOOL – PRIVATE. Joyfully she ran through the gate and up to the top of the nearest sand dune. She was free – she was back in the outside world! There was the bay spread before her, with deck chairs, and ice cream wrappers blowing about and a sprinkling of holiday-makers.

She ran down the other side of the dune and left her bag and socks and shoes at the bottom. Then she sprinted across the hard, golden sand barefoot, past a game of beach cricket, to the far distant sea. Her hair streamed out in the breeze and, because she loved running, she felt exhilarated. She paddled at the water's edge, squeezing wet sand through her toes and letting the salt water run over them. Enviously she watched some surfers. After some time, she walked slowly back across the sands to where she had left her things.

Sitting down at the foot of the sand dune, Rebecca took a thick notepad and ballpoint pen from her bag, filled with the urge to write something. She would make some notes of her first impressions of Trebizon, just like a real writer. She was safe here; nobody would ask her what she was writing.

A family came and settled down nearby, with sandwiches and a flask of tea: a London man and his wife with their two teenage daughters. The girls wore bikinis and found a sheltered hollow to sunbathe in. They hardly gave Rebecca a second glance.

She sat with her knees up, her notepad propped against them, wondering what to write. Her mood of exhilaration had been short-lived. The voices of the family nearby reminded her of London and made her feel homesick. Imperceptibly, the sun was sinking lower towards the green and white-flecked horizon. The rays of light slanted through the sand dunes, filling Rebecca with an ache.

She remembered the first line of a poem written long ago, and she wrote it down neatly, in block capitals:

> THERE'S A CERTAIN SLANT OF LIGHT, ON
> WINTER AFTERNOONS . . .

She followed this by writing:

> IT FALLS THROUGH THE TREES, LIES HEAVY
> ON THE DUNES

Unaware that one of the sunbathers was now watching her with curiosity, Rebecca decided to add some more. She wrote intently, wrinkling her nose in concentration, whispering the words aloud every so often. Sometimes she crossed words out and put in better ones, but on the whole, the poem came easily – it just seemed to flow from that opening line.

When at last it was finished to her satisfaction, Rebecca read it through and sighed. It was as though a heavy weight had been lifted from her shoulders. Writing the verses had somehow relieved her of the awful melancholy mood which had inspired them. She felt better now.

'She must be at that school,' she heard one of the teenagers comment. 'Bet she's brainy.'

Rebecca rummaged in her bag, lowering her eyes.

'It's famous, isn't it? Bet they have a marvellous time there.'

'Helen, Melissa!' That was the father's voice. 'Put something on, let's get back to the caravan before it gets cold.'

Startled, Rebecca looked up at the sky. The warmth was going from the sun. What was the time? How long had she been here? She scrambled into her shoes and socks and dropped her notepad and pen into her bag, first ripping out the page of verse. She read it for the last time, and smiled. Silly, gloomy poem!

'Stop feeling sorry for yourself!' she thought. 'It's *not* a prison. It's one of the best schools in England, and you've got to make a go of it. Mum and Dad expect it.'

There was a litter basket only ten yards away. She walked over to it and pushed her poem down between the squash cartons, cigarette packets and ice cream wrappers that filled the basket. Time to get back to school – to get unpacked – to meet the other girls in her dormitory! Maybe even tea time! She raced up to the top of the sand dune and down the other side, leaving her poem crushed amongst the litter. Dead and buried – best forgotten!

But although Rebecca's poem was buried, it was not dead, nor was it to be forgotten.

FOUR

THE MIGHTY EDITOR

As Rebecca let herself in through the small gate that said
TREBIZON SCHOOL – PRIVATE, the holiday-makers had
gathered their things together and were ready to leave the
beach.

'What on earth are you rummaging around in that dirty
litter basket for, Helen!' asked her father.

'I want to see what she was writing!'

'Come along at once, Helen!' said her mother. 'And put
that piece of paper back!'

The family took the grassy track through the sand dunes
that led in an easterly direction to the small caravan site
where they were staying. Helen trailed along behind with
her sister.

'Here, listen to this, Melissa. It's a poem. I told you she
looked brainy.'

She started reading bits out loud, and giggling.

There was someone coming along the track towards
them, head lowered, deep in thought. Elizabeth Exton, just
like Rebecca, had felt the need to be alone. She had been out
for a long walk, turning over and over in her mind a small

33

problem that went with being the new Editor of *The Trebizon Journal*. She had enjoyed the summer holidays even more than usual; it had been wonderful to have something really important to do, something that had given her the opportunity of meeting and talking to famous people. Nevertheless, this one small problem remained. It was still not resolved – and now it was time to get back to school.

'Oh, chuck it away, Helen,' said Melissa.

The girl, bored with her find now, fluttered the paper in the air, opened her finger and thumb and let it fly away on the breeze. It fluttered straight down to Elizabeth Exton's feet. She picked it up indignantly. Holiday-makers! Litter bugs!

'Come back here!' she called as the girls passed her on the grassy track.

The girl, Helen, stopped, turned round, and stared at her.

'You dropped this.'

'Did I?'

About to give the girl a lecture, Elizabeth realized that it was a poem, quite a good one. The opening line was really most striking. The girl had obviously just written it.

'It – it's a poem,' said Elizabeth, rather feebly.

'Have it,' said the girl shortly. She turned on her heels and hurried on up the grassy track to catch up with her family.

As Elizabeth Exton walked back to school she read the poem over twice. It was all rather uncanny, she decided, and the more she thought about it, the stranger it seemed.

Meanwhile, Rebecca was racing up the back staircase of Juniper House in panic. A loud bell was clanging over in the dining hall block. Girls were rushing past her down the stairs, nearly knocking her over.

'Tea time!'

'You'll be late!'

'But I haven't even washed or unpacked yet!' thought Rebecca.

She charged through a door on the first landing. The dormitory was identical to her own, but the walls were pale green instead of primrose. Wrong floor! She backed out quickly, ran up another flight of stairs, and there was the right door with the number six on it.

Her trunk stood at the foot of her bed. It was neatly labelled REBECCA MASON, JUNIPER HOUSE, TREBIZON SCHOOL and was waiting to be unpacked.

Someone was standing there, her back turned to the door, surveying the trunk. Otherwise the dormitory was empty.

'Rebecca!' said Tish, turning round. 'Where on earth have you been? I've been looking for you.'

Rebecca was surprised and pleased. 'Down on the beach. So I am with you then?'

'That's my bed over there. Look, the bell's gone for tea –'

'I haven't unpacked –'

'Do it after tea. Quick, have a wash. You've got biro on your face. I'll take you over to the dining hall. Sue's saving us seats on Joss Vining's table, which is a good one.'

There was a mirror and handbasin in the dormitory and Rebecca washed her face and brushed her hair at speed. Her spirits lifted. She would have liked to have Tish Anderson as a special friend, but that was too much to hope for. On the other hand, Tish must quite like her or she would hardly be here now, and she certainly wouldn't have arranged for them to sit at the same table.

'Thanks for waiting for me,' said Rebecca. 'I'd have died if I'd had to walk in late on my own.'

'Sorry I lost you when we got off the coach. Come on.'

They hurried down west staircase and out on to the

35

terrace overlooking the quadrangle gardens. At the far end of the terrace, the modern white block that rən at right angles to the boarding house had its french windows open on the ground floor. A deep, continuous hum floated out, like the hum of thousands of wild bees swarming round nectar on a June evening. The girls of Trebizon School were in the dining hall and settling down to tea.

'Race you!' said Tish.

Rebecca hurtled along the terrace, which ran the length of the building, long legs fully stretched. She almost crashed into the wall of the white building at the end.

'Won!'

'You're fast!'

They walked – out of breath – into the big dining hall, where girls sat ten to a table. Josselyn Vining was at the head of their table serving grilled sausages and bacon from a large casserole dish onto plates.

'Sorry we're late, Rebecca got lost.'

'You're the new girl, are you? Hallo. Sausage or bacon or both?'

'Both, please,' said Rebecca hungrily.

'She's a good runner.' Tish looked at Rebecca, who was now piling runner beans onto her plate. 'Sliced tomatoes? Here, Joss was head of games last term and though she doesn't know it, she's going to be again.'

There was laughter round the table, and general approval.

'Good at hockey?' asked Joss.

'I – I don't know,' mumbled Rebecca.

Rebecca knew that she was a good runner. Although she would quite like to be good at organized games, she had not played them very much up till now, except netball.

'Well, if you can run that's a start.'

Sue Murdoch, who was sitting on the other side of Josselyn, said something then about hockey fixtures; Tish joined in, and quickly the three of them fell into animated conversation.

Rebecca felt an elbow nudging her ribs and for the first time became aware of the girl sitting on the other side of her. She had brown hair and a pretty, full-lipped face.

'You watch out,' she said in a conspiratorial whisper. 'You don't want to get in with the sporty brigade. Early morning runs before breakfast, extra hockey practice at weekends . . . once they think you're any good, there's no escape.'

'Thanks for the warning,' smiled Rebecca. It was nice to find someone being so friendly. At the same time, she felt a pang. She would like to be one of that little group talking about fixtures. They had obviously been in a junior team together last year, and travelled to other schools for matches. 'Do they really take it all that seriously?'

'You bet they do,' said the girl with feeling.

At that moment Rebecca saw Tish throw back her head and laugh about something, her mouth even wider than usual, her black curls bouncing. Did Tish go for runs before breakfast, too?

'Don't worry,' the girl was saying now, 'there's plenty of us who are normal here. I'm Debbie Rickard by the way – your name's Rebecca, isn't it?'

Although Rebecca did not know it at the time, Debbie Rickard was exaggerating wildly, and her attitude was coloured by the fact that she herself was hopeless at games of any kind.

She was happy to talk to Debbie for the rest of the meal; the girl was going out of her way to be friendly. Besides, everybody seemed to want to talk to Tish Anderson. When they had finished their fresh fruit and yoghurt, the Greek girl, Mara Leonodis, came over from the next table and grabbed the back of Tish's jumper.

'I've seen Miss Morgan!' she said. 'She's got a staff meeting after tea but she says she'll meet us in the Hobbies' Room later and arrange where we're to put it.'

'Good!' said Tish, obviously excited.

Rebecca thought again of the big carton that Mara had brought to school, containing some kind of 'machine'. What was it?

There was a deafening noise of scraping chairs all over the dining hall as girls started to disperse. Josselyn Vining was asking Sally Elphinstone to have a game of badminton with her, and Tish was deep in conversation with Mara Leonodis. Sue Murdoch said she was going to 'the Hilary', wherever that was.

'What are you going to do now?' asked Debbie.

'I've still got to unpack my trunk.'

'I'll come with you.'

In the dormitory, Rebecca soon sorted out her things. She placed her clothes neatly in the drawers of the pink chest and hung up her dressing gown. Her personal possessions she put in the locker beside her bed.

'Your trunk goes outside on the landing with the others,' said Debbie, dragging it out through the door. 'They'll collect them up soon and put them in store till the end of term. Your outdoor things –' she pointed to Wellington boots, raincoat and school cape, '– go downstairs. And there's a special locker for all your games stuff.'

Debbie helped her carry the clothes downstairs and showed her where to put them. Rebecca was very grateful for all this. But when Debbie dragged her along the corridor on the ground floor to a small room with a television set in it,

Rebecca pulled up short in the doorway. It was a nice evening and she didn't want to watch TV.

'I think I'd quite like to look round the grounds,' she said.

'But it's "Landslide"!' protested Debbie.

'Then don't miss it for me!' said Rebecca. 'I'll be fine.'

'Are you sure?' Debbie looked relieved. 'I'll see you later then – see you at cocoa time.'

As the door closed and Rebecca was left standing in the corridor, a voice behind her said, 'Come on, I'll give you a guided tour.'

'Oh –' Rebecca turned and saw Tish. 'Will you really?'

They went outside. Although the main school buildings were grouped around the quadrangle, there were other buildings in the grounds, too.

'That big white place in the trees is the sports centre. We hire it out quite a bit to help pay for the upkeep. It's got an indoor swimming pool, badminton, squash, the lot.' Tish kept up a fast pace. 'There's the hockey pitches, and the grass tennis courts – the hard courts are the other side of the sports centre, and we use them for netball this term. Come and look at the lake –'

They galloped along a flagstone path, through a shrubbery, and came out by water. The 'lake' was really a large pond, very reedy and beautiful with water lilies floating upon it. Beside the water stood a long low building; it had once been mews cottages and a coach-house, now modernized with plate glass windows, and a Spanish-style verandah overlooking the water. The whole scene was most attractive. Through the open windows came the strains of music, floating across the water.

'That's the Hilary,' explained Tish. 'The Hilary Camberwell Music School where we have our music lessons and people learn to play instruments. There are lots of little practice rooms. That violin you can hear might be Sue.'

On they went in a breathless whirl; it was really too much for Rebecca's mind to take in all at once. There were some very attractive houses set at various points in the grounds. Some, Tish explained, were staff houses and the larger ones were boarding houses for the Third Years upwards.

'After Juniper we go into smaller houses, thirty or forty girls, more free and easy, with shared studies. All the boarding houses have names – Willoughby, Chambers, Parkinson – you won't remember them yet. Look, there's Parkinson, that's the Upper Sixth's boarding house.'

They slowed down as they passed close to an attractive old Victorian house with large bay windows and walls covered in ivy. It had its own garden, with garden seats and a summerhouse. Somebody came out of the side gate and they stopped to let her cross their path. Rebecca at once recognized the tall, elegant figure with the striking bony features and long black hair. Her hair streamed out behind her. There was something rather witch-like about Elizabeth Exton when you looked at her from the side.

'Elizabeth?'

'What do you want Ishbel?' asked the prefect touchily. She was obviously in a hurry.

'How long have I got to collect Juniper's contributions, please?'

Rebecca thought she saw an annoyed frown cross the prefect's face; but, if so, it was quickly gone.

'About a fortnight. It'll be announced in Assembly. Are you still Magazine Officer then?'

'Yes, we're elected for two terms. It won't give the new girls much time. We had about four weeks last year when we were new.'

'New girls don't expect to get in the *Journal*, surely?'

'Two got in last year when Mary Green was Editor.'

'Well, just guess who's the Editor of *The Trebizon Journal* now – and it's not Mary Green.' Her eyes swept over Rebecca for a moment. She was about to say something, and then changed her mind. She spoke more reasonably. 'It goes to press early because it's the Golden Jubilee edition, remember? I'm sorry I can't give you longer. Everything will be considered on its merits.'

She hurried on her way.

'Piffling juniors,' she said, under her breath.

FIVE

THE BOX IS OPENED

'Come on,' said Tish, crisply. 'I'd better get notices up straight away. Seen round Juniper yet?'

Rebecca shook her head.

'Well, you can see it now.'

They hurried back to the red brick boarding house, went inside and along the corridor.

'This end of the building is the west wing, where all the Second Years live – the other end is the east wing, for the First Years. It's really two boarding houses in one building, joined by this corridor on the ground floor. This is our Hobbies' Room.'

She pushed open a modern glass door, like the one leading to the TV room. But unlike the tiny TV room, this was huge and airy, about the length of two classrooms. It was crammed with interesting things.

Rebecca noticed a table tennis table, a sewing table with two sewing machines on it and a potter's wheel. There was an Art corner with easels and a sink with a shelf of empty jam jars and poster paints above.

Then Rebecca saw the typewriter. It was on a table under

the window. Tish went over, sat down and fed in two sheets of typing paper with carbon paper in between them and rapidly typed some sentences.

'You can type!' exclaimed Rebecca.

'My sister's taught me,' said Tish, pulling the sheets out. 'A few mistakes, but not bad. I'm going to need to be able to type. Come on, we'll put one notice in the First Year Common Room and the carbon copy in ours.'

Rebecca's legs were beginning to feel weary and she would very much like to have stayed and tinkered with that typewriter, but she followed Tish out along the corridor, the length of the building, up east staircase and into the First Year Common Room.

It was a lovely light room on the first floor, overlooking the quadrangle gardens, with comfortable chairs, rugs on the floor, two tables and a piano in the corner. There was a large notice-board by the door. Tish took a spare drawing pin off the board and pinned up her notice. Rebecca read it with interest:

Urgent. *Magazine Meeting 7 pm tomorrow (Wednesday) in the Second Year Common Room. Contributions for this term's* Trebizon Journal *required by next Monday. If you have anything suitable please bring it with you tomorrow. This will be the Golden Jubilee edition and we want our House represented.*

Ishbel Anderson *Magazine Officer*
Juniper House

'Pity there's no-one here to read it at the moment!' said Tish.

'Where are they all?' asked Rebecca, suddenly realizing. 'The place is deserted.'

'Most likely over in the library getting a pep talk from the Head. That's where we went on our first evening. She likes to see all the new girls when they arrive. Looks 'em over!'

'Then –?'

'Don't worry, you'll get a message when she wants to see you,' said Tish. 'And don't look so scared. She's nice, really nice. Come on, you can see our Common Room now, it's just like this.'

They doubled back down east staircase, right along the ground floor corridor and up west. Tish threw open the door of the Second Year Common Room.

'Hi, Tish!'

'How are you?'

Girls were lounging around in chairs and some were lying on the rugs on the floor, reading. They crowded round the notice as it was pinned up. The notice-board was usually a great focal point of interest in their school life.

'The kitchen's just opposite, like to see it?' asked Tish, leading Rebecca out into the corridor. 'We make tea and coffee there, and our own cocoa at bed-time –'

She got no further. A tall, pretty girl of seventeen appeared at the top of the staircase. She was a prefect called Pippa Fellowes-Walker.

'Rebecca?' she asked. 'Rebecca Mason?'

Rebecca nodded, feeling scared.

'Run upstairs and wash, and brush your hair. I'll wait for you here. Miss Welbeck will see you in ten minutes.'

Rebecca's throat felt dry. She bolted upstairs. Summoned to see the Principal of Trebizon School! She collected her wash things from the dormitory and found a big wash room right next door. There was a long row of wash basins and a row of hooks to hang flannels on. There was also a toothbrush rack with brush handles hanging down all colours of the rainbow, and just one slot free for her own new, bright blue toothbrush.

When she returned to the landing below she found the prefect chatting amiably with Tish, not at all god-like and superior: not like Elizabeth Exton. She gave Rebecca a friendly smile. 'You'll do! Come on, follow me.'

Pippa liked the look of this new girl with the fair hair and the delicate features; there was something intelligent, and artistic-looking about her.

They went downstairs and out onto the terrace and crossed the quadrangle gardens to the back of the old school. Pippa took Rebecca in through the same glass door that she had passed through earlier with Miss Morgan, and back into that awe-inspiring entrance hall with its magnificent muralled staircase.

On the first floor, the prefect knocked on an oak-panelled door, and then looked into the room. Then she came out and spoke quietly.

'Miss Welbeck will see you now. Find your own way back? Okay. In you go.'

Afterwards, Rebecca always got a pleasant glow when she recalled that first meeting with Miss Madeleine Welbeck. Within moments of entering the panelled study, filled with the scent of roses, her fear left her. She saw a slim woman in tweeds, standing by a large window overlooking the entrance forecourt, watching a car drive off. She caught a glimpse of oak trees and park land in the distance and here in the room the evening light catching Miss Welbeck's fair-to-silver hair as she turned.

'Welcome to Trebizon, Rebecca.'

Rebecca felt herself to be in the presence of someone quiet and confident whom she could admire. She found Miss Welbeck had a tremendous effect on her, and when she emerged from her study, ten minutes later, she felt quite inspired. The Principal's last words were still ringing in her ears.

'Aim high, Rebecca. Don't expect success to come too easily, but keep on reaching up. Remember: "Two men looked through the prison bars, one saw mud and the other saw stars". Don't look down at the mud but reach up for the stars.'

What a clever thing to say! That bit about prison bars – could Miss Welbeck possibly have guessed how Rebecca had been feeling earlier? Reach up for the stars! Yes – why not? Why shouldn't she?

She walked down the magnificent staircase, gazing up at the richly coloured murals. She no longer felt overwhelmed by it, but inspired. Small and insignificant though she was, she must make her mark at Trebizon School, and justify her presence.

'Write something for that magazine!' had been her father's last words to her. What an honour it would be if she could get something printed in the Golden Jubilee edition of *The Trebizon Journal*! Of course, thinking of the mighty Elizabeth Exton, that wasn't just aiming high – it was aiming for the moon. But why not try? Why not?

When Rebecca re-entered Juniper House she heard a hubbub of voices echoing along the corridor, coming from the direction of the Hobbies' Room. The door was open and it sounded as though there was quite a crowd in there. What was going on? She decided to find out!

They were all gathered round the big table by the window, the typewriter table. There was a large carton near the door, its packing removed. Rebecca recognized it as the mysterious box that Mara had brought back to school with her. Miss Morgan and Tish had carried something over to the table and set it down next to the typewriter, and Mara was dusting it with a cloth.

'It's smashing!' said Josselyn Vining, tapping Mara on the shoulder with her badminton racquet. 'Do you mean to say your father didn't want it?'

'We were all expecting some grotty old thing!' laughed Tish. 'And Mara turns up with this.'

'It was down in the Southampton Office,' said Mara, with great pleasure. Her father was the owner of Leonodis Shipping Lines. 'It was much too small for them and now they have a new one as big –' Mara spread her arms out, '– as big as this.'

Rebecca's curiosity was at fever pitch – what was it? She stood on tip-toe behind the other girls and at last she could see. A duplicating machine! Just a little, hand-operated model, but quite modern. Beside it were boxes of stencils and duplicating paper, all that was required to put it into action.

'I think this is the best place, next to the typewriter,' said Miss Morgan. 'Now this corner of the Hobbies' Room can be your publishing office! I look forward to seeing what you publish!'

So saying, Miss Morgan moved away and, as the crowd parted to let her through, she walked past Rebecca and smiled and went over to the doorway. Before leaving, she called back, 'Cocoa time in ten minutes!'

'Yes, Miss Morgan,' responded the girls, already closing round the duplicator again.

Rebecca was beginning to feel quite excited. A miniature publishing office – what fun! – and what *were* they going to publish?

Even as she mentally asked that question, Tish jumped up on to a chair and answered it. 'Well, this is it! I've been practising typing in the holidays to be able to type the stencils. Mara has turned up with the machine, just as she said she would. From now on we can produce our own House publication – *The Juniper Journal*!'

'Hurray!' There was cheering and stamping of feet.

'I'll announce it properly at the magazine meeting tomorrow. We'll make it the best thing in the school –' She was interrupted by more cheers, but ended on a modest note. 'Except for *The Trebizon Journal* itself, of course.'

As Rebecca came out of the Hobbies' Room with a bunch of other girls, she was met by Debbie Rickard in the corridor. Debbie immediately put her arm through Rebecca's.

'Hallo! I've been looking for you. Where've you been?'

'I had to go and see the Principal.'

'Come and have cocoa, I'll show you where we make it.'

They made cocoa in the big warm kitchen on the first floor and sat and drank it, munching two digestive biscuits. Drinking cocoa, either in the kitchen or in the comfortable Common Room across the corridor, was a nightly ritual at Trebizon School.

'How did you get on with the Principal?'

'Fine,' said Rebecca, hugging to herself her secret resolve to make something of herself at her new school. 'She's nice.'

Debbie Rickard was in a different dormitory from Rebecca, but they were to be in the same form, II Alpha. Before they parted, Debbie said, 'Shall we sit next to each other in lessons tomorrow?'

'I'd like that,' said Rebecca gratefully. Tomorrow would be her first full day at Trebizon and she was pleased that she would not have to face it alone. She had already made a friend, of sorts.

She went up to her dormitory. When she had said

goodbye to her parents that morning, Rebecca had been dreading her first night at boarding school. She imagined that she might toss and turn all night in her strange surroundings, feeling terribly homesick. In fact, she lay in bed and tried to plan what she would write for the school magazine. Her eyelids got heavier and heavier.

All round her, girls were whispering and running about and discussing the holidays, until the duty prefect came in and said in a stern voice, 'Shut up! Lights out!'

But Rebecca knew nothing of this, for she was already fast asleep.

SIX

DEBBIE IS SPITEFUL

The first full day at Trebizon, Wednesday, Rebecca still did not feel a twinge of homesickness. The hours were too crowded for that and, in the few quiet times, she had something special to keep her thoughts occupied: her secret resolve to try and write something for *The Trebizon Journal*.

After the rising bell went, she knelt up on her pillow and pulled back the curtains. She stared in surprise at the trees and blue sea beyond and just for a moment wondered where she was.

Girls were hurrying to and from the wash room; some were already scrambling into their clothes.

'Where's my tie?' shouted someone.

'Hallo, Rebecca,' said a girl in a pale green dressing gown, with sandy hair, passing the foot of the bed. 'Sleep well?'

'Fine, thanks.'

It was only after she had gone that Rebecca realized the girl was Sue Murdoch, without her glasses. Spectacles suited her well, but without them she looked entirely different. She had rather a Slavonic face, with high cheekbones.

Rebecca could just imagine her on the platform in a big concert hall, playing the violin, when she was grown up.

Rebecca washed and dressed in a hurry, but she was still brushing her hair when Tish and Sue came past.

'Buck up! Breakfast in five minutes. You're on Joss Vining's table – where you sat last night, remember? Okay?'

Rebecca would have liked them to have waited for her, but told herself not to be such a baby. She went down and entered the dining hall with a throng of other girls; at least she wasn't late! She found the right table and an empty seat, next to Sally Elphinstone this time. To her regret, Tish was right at the other end of the table, talking madly as usual.

'Why's the seat next to me always left till last?' asked Sally in mock dismay. 'As if I didn't know.'

'You should go on a diet, Elf,' said Judy Sharp. 'Don't let her squeeze you off the table, Rebecca.'

'There's plenty of room!' laughed Rebecca, and turning said, 'Is that what they call you – Elf –?'

'That's right, because of my elfin figure,' said the plump girl cheerfully. 'Elfin Elphinstone, that's me. Help yourself to cereal and the milk's in the big jug. Oi – Tish – don't take all the muesli, pass it up this way. I'm fading away.'

Rebecca ate a hearty breakfast. There was much chatter and laughter on her table and so theirs was one of the last to finish. She was still eating toast when Debbie Rickard passed by from another table. Although she had sat there on the first evening, Joss Vining's table was not Debbie's proper one.

'Don't forget, Rebecca! We'll sit together in lessons.' She bent her head close for a second. 'See you after Assembly.'

Rebecca's pleasure was slightly marred by the look on Elf's face as she watched Debbie walk on. What was the plump girl raising her eyebrows about?

The assembly hall was immediately above the dining hall, and had a very high ceiling. Outside the french windows on either side of the hall, balconies ran its entire length. As the girls filed in, a mistress played stirring music on a grand piano.

When the whole school was assembled, the music stopped and the rows of girls stood silent as a figure entered. Miss Welbeck walked the length of the hall, her black gown flapping, went up on to the stage and stood behind a table. She placed her hymn book and some notices on the polished surface beside a bowl of chrysanthemums, then gazed around the hall.

'Good morning, girls.'

'Good morning, Miss Welbeck.'

The Principal of Trebizon School had arrived to take Assembly and the new school year had officially begun.

After Assembly, Rebecca was pleased to discover that most lessons took place in the old building, the 18th century manor house that formed the heart of the school. The science laboratories and home economics rooms were in the modern part of school, but the form rooms were in the old building and II Alpha was a quaint room with sloping, uneven floors and old-fashioned windows.

There were nine double desks in three rows in the room and Rebecca sat next to Debbie in the front row. Of the other sixteen girls in her form, Rebecca recognized several from her dining table, including Tish, Sue, Joss Vining, Judy Sharp and Sally Elphinstone and two more from her dormitory. She would soon get to know the others. Mara Leonodis was not there.

She liked Miss Heath, her form-mistress, at once and soon discovered that she also took them for English, Rebecca's favourite subject. At the end of the English lesson

Miss Heath said, 'Now for your prep. I want an essay written, please. All essays will be handed in on Friday morning. Here are the subjects.'

She chalked them up on the blackboard:

A WINTER'S MORNING.
MY ADVENTURE IN SPACE.
THE QUARREL.

The girls scribbled the headings down in their rough books as Miss Heath left the room. The maths mistress was waiting outside.

'Which one will you do?' asked Debbie.

'The first one,' replied Rebecca at once. She was glad they had until Friday to write the essay; today was only Wednesday. She wanted to make it really good. Once again her mind went back to her interview with the Principal, and her resolve to try and make her mark at her new school.

'Coming to watch TV?' asked Debbie after tea.

'I'm going to write my essay,' said Rebecca.

'But you can do it tomorrow night!' said Debbie in surprise. She always left her prep as long as possible. So did Rebecca, but only when the subject didn't interest her. 'Besides, you might miss the magazine meeting, if you're interested in that sort of thing.'

'I'll be back in time for that!' said Rebecca confidently.

'See you there, then.'

Rebecca wouldn't have missed the magazine meeting for anything. She would have liked to explain to Debbie that she wanted to make a start on her English essay because then, tomorrow, she might have time to start thinking about what she could write for *The Trebizon Journal*. But she said nothing; she had the feeling that Debbie might laugh at her for being so ambitious.

In the quiet peace of the library, Rebecca wrote her essay in rough. Older girls had studies in their boarding houses, but younger girls were required to do prep in their form rooms or in the school library. Since discovering the library during the course of the day, there had been no question in Rebecca's mind.

It was a beautiful room, the library of the original manor house, with some rare books housed there. French windows led out on to the terrace, overlooking the main forecourt of the school with a fine view of park land beyond. She worked out that Miss Welbeck's study must be immediately above the library. Occasionally, cars drew up as people came and went from the school and here Rebecca somehow felt in touch with the outside world.

It was nearly seven o'clock when she finished her essay. She could touch it up later, and copy it into her brand new English exercise book, but now she must go to the magazine meeting!

The Second Year Common Room was packed out with both First and Second Years, and Tish was kneeling up on a chair to take the meeting. There was a wire basket on the table beside her.

'This meeting is really to tell First Years about the school magazine, and how things are selected for it, and also to collect contributions from Second Years, who've had all the holidays to do something.'

Tish then quickly explained how her position as Magazine Officer made her a 'mini editor' of *The Trebizon Journal*, just as she had explained it to Rebecca on the train journey down.

'So you First Years have still got a few days,' she ended.

'But I must have everything in by eight o'clock next Monday evening, that's the final deadline. I'll be sitting in here from seven o'clock onwards. You, too, Rebecca –' she added, catching her eye encouragingly. 'You've still got time.'

Debbie nudged Rebecca hard. 'She's got a hope!' she whispered, and Rebecca went red. She had been quite uplifted by Tish's encouragement. She was glad, very glad, that she had confided nothing of her secret ambition to Debbie.

'We'll have another meeting next Wednesday,' Tish was saying. 'Same time, same place. I'll have a short list of the best entries and we'll pass them round and vote. The best one will be gold starred and one or two others will go up as well. Okay? Now, Second Years come and put your stuff in this basket – but nobody go yet, please.'

Girls shuffled up with their poems, essays and drawings and placed them in the wire basket. Roberta Jones hung back till last and then strode up and slapped her poems on top of the pile, looking satisfied. Now Tish would have to read hers first!

'The other thing I want to talk about is *The Juniper Journal*. We're going to have our own house publication this term. Even if you don't get anything in the school magazine, and most of you won't, we're going to need lots of stuff for *The J.J.* Verses, jokes, items of news. Be thinking about it. As soon as we've done our best, as far as this term's school magazine is concerned, we'll get *The J.J.* organized. That means a meeting some time next week to elect an editor and committee. I'll put a notice up in both Common Rooms.'

'Tish for Editor!' shouted Mara Leonodis, and the meeting broke up with clapping, laughter, and noise.

The word was passed round about the duplicator that had

arrived in the Second Year Hobbies' Room. Several of the new First Year girls rushed off to look at it.

'Thinks she's the Queen of England,' said Debbie suddenly, as they walked down the corridor. 'Tish Anderson, I mean.'

Rebecca was quite startled by the touch of venom.

As she got into bed that night, Tish came past in her dressing gown and stood for a moment at the foot of the bed. She had just cleaned her teeth and with her wide smile she looked rather like a toothpaste advertisement. 'I'm glad you came to the meeting. Going to try and do something for *The Trebizon*?'

'Yes,' Rebecca blurted out. 'As a matter of fact, I am!'

'Good.'

'I know – from what Elizabeth Exton said – that there isn't much chance. But there's no harm in trying.'

'There's not much chance but there's always *some* chance,' said Tish. Then very casually, 'Do you like Debbie Rickard?'

'Why, yes,' said Rebecca. 'She – she's fine.'

'Hockey tomorrow afternoon,' said Tish, changing the subject. 'I've forgotten – have you played before?'

'Hardly at all. I know the rules, and that's about all.'

'Well, you ought to be good.'

Rebecca knew that she was referring, once again, to the race they had run together when they had been late for tea yesterday. As she went to sleep she made up her mind to try and do well in the lesson tomorrow – she would try and be good at hockey! After all, if she wanted to get noticed at Trebizon it was no use pinning *all* her hopes on getting something published in the school magazine!

But the hockey lesson next day was a washout as far as Rebecca could see. She was given a red sash to wear by Miss

Willis, the games mistress, and put into a full-scale hockey game straight away, reds verses blues. The position chosen for her was left back, with Debbie Rickard playing at right back.

'Isn't this the biggest bore of all time?' said Debbie, as they hung around their end of the draughty field with only the goalkeeper for company. There was a biting east wind today.

'Yes,' said Rebecca, running up and down on the spot to keep warm. 'It is.'

The trouble was that reds had Josselyn Vining at centre forward, supported by Tish Anderson and Sue Murdoch at left and right inner, and the three of them made a winning combination. They attacked the opposing goal time and time again and the red defence had almost nothing to do. On a few occasions that the ball came her way, Rebecca was too cold and miserable to stop it in time.

As she watched the dazzling stick work and passing going on amongst the red forwards, Rebecca wondered how she could have been insane enough to think she might be good at hockey.

'And what does Tish Anderson look like in a games skirt!' giggled Debbie, after they had changed ends at half-time.

'Well, she's got thick legs for a start,' said Rebecca, feeling jaundiced. 'I suppose that's what playing hockey does for you.'

Rebecca did not mean the remark spitefully. In fact she had been surprised to notice that Tish had very thick, muscular legs when the rest of her was quite slim and graceful. She regretted the remark as soon as she had made it, especially when Debbie went off into peals of laughter.

'It's not that funny,' she said irritably.

Only once did Rebecca get a chance to warm up. The

opposing centre forward, Judy Sharp, came streaking through just before the end of the game and hit the ball a mighty whack with her hockey stick. It missed the goal and went racing away into the distance. The game came to a stop while Rebecca streaked off to retrieve the ball, running flat out all the way and just getting her stick to it before it rolled into a ditch full of brambles. Glad to get warm, she ran back with it all the way, tapping it ahead of her as she ran.

She would have been surprised if she could have looked upfield and seen the sudden interest on Josselyn Vining's face.

'Did you see that, Tish?'

'I told you she could run.'

That evening, some time after tea, Tish came into the TV room.

'Could you find Rebecca please, Debbie?' she asked. She was wearing a track suit, and as she was acting on the instructions of the hockey captain she was allowed to order people around, within reason. 'Tell her to be on school pitch with her hockey things in ten minutes for a trial game.'

Debbie was amazed, and deeply envious. She got to her feet. 'She won't come!' she burst out. 'She hates hockey. And do you know what she told me today? She said you've got thick legs because you play so much hockey, and she doesn't want to look like you.'

As Tish coloured deeply, Debbie felt a touch of satisfaction. 'But of course I'll tell her that Joss wants her,' she said sweetly. 'I'm just warning you that she probably won't turn up.'

SEVEN

END OF A FRIENDSHIP

Rebecca was in her favourite place, the library, and Debbie failed to find her. She looked into the Common Room on the first floor, then came back down and looked into the Hobbies' Room. She was alarmed to see from the clock on the wall that it was almost time for her favourite quiz programme on the TV.

'She must be doing her prep in the form room!' she thought and raced out and across the quadrangle gardens to the old school.

But of course Rebecca was not there either.

'Well, I've done my best,' thought Debbie virtuously, as she returned to the TV room and switched on the set. She picked up her English exercise book and ballpoint pen from a table and carried on writing, with half an eye on the programme. 'As if Rebecca would want to turn out, anyway. She'll be glad I couldn't find her.'

With that, Debbie put the whole matter right out of her mind.

In the library, Rebecca had her thick notepad open, the one she kept for her private writing, and was struggling with some lines of verse. If she were going to submit something for the school magazine, it had better be good. But – 'Awful', she groaned, when she read over her work.

She realized that the poem she had written on the beach had been better, although rather melancholy. But she couldn't remember it properly now, and besides, she wouldn't want to submit that for obvious reasons. She consoled herself with the thought that she had until Monday and it was still only Thursday. She would give up for tonight and turn her attention to her English essay instead.

She read through 'A Winter's Morning' and felt altogether more satisfied. It wasn't bad, but there were ways it could be improved. She spent a long time on the rough copy, changing words and phrases. Then, with a sigh of satisfaction she copied it out carefully in her best book and blotted it.

'Rebecca!' said an astonished voice. 'Have you seen the time?'

It was the prefect, Pippa Fellowes-Walker, who was on library duty that evening. She had only just noticed Rebecca, hidden behind a bookcase, working away as quiet as a mouse.

'Oh!' said Rebecca, looking at the clock. 'I've missed cocoa.'

'You certainly have,' said Pippa. 'You're supposed to be in bed in five minutes. You're not supposed to spend as long as this on prep! Go on – off you go!'

Rebecca rushed back to the boarding house and almost collided with Tish coming out of the wash room in pyjamas and dressing gown and ready for bed. 'Hallo!' she said. 'I missed cocoa –'

She got no further, for Tish walked straight past her in

stony silence. A coldness gripped Rebecca. What was the matter? What had she done wrong?

She was even more alarmed the following morning to find that both Tish and Sue were completely ignoring her, passing by her bed without a word, and hurrying down to breakfast together. Josselyn Vining was in a different dormitory but when Rebecca sat at the table in the dining hall, it struck her that Joss, too, seemed to be looking straight through her with a cold expression on her face.

Rebecca ate her cornflakes, feeling unhappy and confused. Were they being cool to her? Or was she imagining things? Was it simply that they had gone out of their way to be friendly because she was new, and now that she was settling in and had found a friend, they felt they didn't have to bother any more.

Whatever the reason, it cast a cloud over her entire day. Even the satisfaction of handing in her essay to Miss Heath was marred by her general feeling of unease.

As though to compensate for the unfriendliness of the other girls, Debbie Rickard was more friendly than ever before, as they sat together in lessons. Instead of finding this a comfort, Rebecca found that Debbie's constant chatter was beginning to get on her nerves.

'Please stop talking, Rebecca!' said Miss Gates, the maths mistress, turning round from the blackboard, and Rebecca went bright red. She hadn't been talking – Debbie had!

'Sorry,' whispered Debbie a little later.

The last lesson of the day was netball. This, at least, was a game that Rebecca had played many times before – not only at her London comprehensive school, but at her primary school before that. She was no good as a shooter but was very fast and useful in centre court positions. Unfortunately, as in the hockey game the previous day, she was put in a defence position.

Nevertheless, Rebecca had nothing to distract her, for Debbie Rickard was playing on another court, and she did her best. Although she was playing in her least favourite position she was fast on to the ball, and several times prevented Josselyn Vining getting hold of it in the shooting circle. This was tantamount to preventing goals, for Joss was the opposing shooter and every time she got the ball in the circle a goal would follow as sure as day follows night.

'I wonder if she hates netball, too?' Rebecca heard Joss say to Tish after the game.

'I expect so.'

'Pity.'

Rebecca, who had very sharp ears, saw them glance in her direction and knew at once that they had been referring to her. She could not bear their cold looks and, now, the growing feeling that something strange was going on. She walked over to them.

'I don't hate netball,' she blurted out. 'Why should I?'

'Well, you hate hockey, don't you?'

'Who told you that?'

'Your friend Debbie Rickard. It's true, isn't it?'

'I – I –' Rebecca broke off, feeling confused. It was certainly true that she had not enjoyed that first game yesterday, and she had told Debbie so.

She finished, lamely, 'I don't know yet whether I like it or not.'

She hurried away from the courts to the changing rooms in the sports centre. As she took a shower, various thoughts passed through her head. At last, she felt, she had some clue to Tish's cool behaviour. But it still didn't make sense. She felt a growing anger towards Debbie that she had told the others that she – Rebecca – 'hated' hockey, but she also felt sure that neither Tish nor Joss were the sort to lose much sleep over *that*. There must be more to it.

'What else has Debbie been saying?' wondered Rebecca.

When she got back to school, she found Debbie sitting on the terrace overlooking the quandrangle gardens, reading a book.

'Hallo, where have you been?' she asked Rebecca.

'Having a shower.'

'I can't bear showers,' said Debbie, screwing up her nose. 'Here, come and sit down. Tea bell should be going in a minute.'

But Rebecca did not sit down. She stood over Debbie. 'Why did you tell Josselyn Vining that I hate hockey?'

'I haven't even seen Joss Vining.'

'Well, Tish Anderson, then,' said Rebecca. Her feeling of uneasiness was growing every minute. 'How did it happen?'

'Oh, yes,' Debbie frowned, remembering. 'Tish was trying to rake you out for some game last night. She asked me to find you, but I told her you wouldn't want to play.'

'You might have asked me!' exclaimed Rebecca.

'I looked for you everywhere, absolutely everywhere!' said Debbie indignantly. 'I meant to tell you this morning, but I forgot. I'd have thought you'd be glad I couldn't find you.'

Rebecca realized that this must have been when she was in the library the previous evening; but her thoughts were already moving on with lightning speed.

'What else did you tell Tish?' she asked fiercely.

'Well,' Debbie started to laugh, but now that she could see the expression on Rebecca's face, the laughter was rather forced. 'I told her just what you thought of her legs and –'

'You *what?*'

'What's the matter with you?' said Debbie irritably. 'You thought it was funny enough yesterday. It's about time she was cut down to size. She's so full of herself, thinks she's so popular and that everybody likes her –'

'But I like her, too!' said Rebecca. 'And if she is popular she can't help that, any more than she can help having thick legs. I think that was really mean and spiteful.'

'Well, you shouldn't have said it then!' snapped Debbie. 'And if you like her so much, why don't you go off and be her friend. If she'll have you, that is,' she ended, with a sneer.

The tea bell sounded.

'I certainly don't want to be *your* friend,' said Rebecca, turning on her heel. 'I'm going.'

She marched off along the terrace towards the dining hall, with tears of anger pricking behind her eyes. So that was what her so-called friend was really like! Now things were beginning to fall into place. She knew why Sally Elphinstone had raised her eyebrows, and why Tish had asked that casual question, 'Do you like Debbie Rickard?' They had been surprised that Rebecca liked Debbie, and no wonder.

'It's better that I've found out now,' Rebecca told herself as she sat down to tea. She was trying to console herself. 'It's better to know sooner than later. Before she gets me into worse trouble.'

Even the fact that she'd been blamed for Debbie's talking in class that morning now caused Rebecca to feel angry. Some friend!

'Better to have no friends at all,' she thought, but at the same time a slight sense of panic overwhelmed her as she thought of the term stretching ahead of her, the many weeks before she would be going home for Christmas and seeing her family and old friends again. It gave her little appetite for tea.

Afterwards she went up to Joss and said awkwardly, 'I'm sorry I didn't turn up last night. I've only just heard about it. Debbie looked for me but wasn't able to find me.'

'Would you have come if you had known in time?' asked Joss.

Rebecca thought very hard. She still imagined that it had been a casual invitation to join in a game of hockey after school. Debbie had not explained to her that it was a trial game and that Joss was already beginning to think about picking the Under Fourteen school team for this season.

'Well, would you have come?' prompted Sue Murdoch, who was standing nearby. 'Honestly?'

Rebecca thought of what she had been doing in the library and how important it had been to her. She shook her head. 'No,' she said truthfully. 'There was something else I wanted to do. But I'd have come over to the pitch and explained.'

'Fair enough,' said Joss.

The two of them went off and joined up with Tish, reporting the conversation to her.

'You must admit she's frank,' said Joss.

'Too frank,' said Tish, with feeling. But she felt a little better towards Rebecca now. 'Trust Debbie Rickard not to bother to look for her properly. Can't think what Rebecca sees in her.'

For her part, Rebecca wished there were some way she could undo the hurt that her unkind remark must have caused Tish, once it had been relayed by Debbie, but it was something that could not be undone.

She went to her favourite place, the library. Somehow she must cling on to her resolve to write something for the school magazine. Drowning in homesickness, that was her one lifeline. She must be able to go home at the end of her first term and show them that she had achieved something: make them proud of her.

But nothing would come.

Rebecca had never found it difficult to compose poems before; she had won prizes for them. But they had never seemed so important before. Now that it really mattered, everything she wrote dissatisfied her.

She spent not only Friday evening, but most of the weekend trying to write the best poem she had ever written. The harder she tried, the worse her verses seemed to become.

She tried in the library, she tried in the school grounds; she even tried to write down on the beach, remembering how easily the words had flowed there when she had first arrived on the Tuesday. All the time she kept well out of Debbie Rickard's way, and everybody else's too. But still nothing would come.

On Sunday afternoon, Tish saw her sitting on the bank of the little lake by the music school, with her notepad on her knees, frowning and deep in concentration. Tish had come to the Hilary to meet Sue after violin practice, and just slipped silently through a side door without Rebecca seeing her. She felt obscurely pleased to see that she was not with Debbie Rickard, and also that she appeared to be writing something.

At bed-time that night she asked Rebecca, 'Got something to hand in to me tomorrow?'

'No.' Rebecca shook her head. 'Sorry.'

She turned and buried her face in her pillow. She was touched that Tish was still nice enough to show an interest, and it made it all ten times worse. Tomorrow was the deadline for handing in magazine entries and she had failed to produce anything. Her one hope of glory was fading away, in front of her eyes. A week of lessons stretched ahead of her, most of them to be spent – oh, horrors – sitting next to Debbie Rickard. Could anything be worse?

Rebecca thought, with longing, of home.

Although she did not know it, her spirits at that moment had reached their lowest ebb. They could sink no further. From now on they could only begin to rise.

EIGHT

JUNIPER VOTES

The first good thing that happened to Rebecca on Monday was supposed to be a 'punishment'. It took place after Miss Heath had called the register on Monday morning.

'Rebecca, Deborah,' said the form-mistress, sternly fixing her gaze on them, 'I have had complaints from three different mistresses about you two, talking during lessons, and I'm afraid I shall have to split you up.'

She looked all round the room at the pairs of girls seated at their double desks, thinking hard. Then she pointed: 'Susan and Ishbel, you tend to chatter rather a lot, too. So I think, let me see, Ishbel can sit in Margot's place at the back, next to Judith. I think it would be a good thing for Margot to come to the front. Margot come forward and sit in Rebecca's place next to Deborah, and you, Rebecca, collect up your books and sit at the back next to Susan.'

Rebecca felt weak all over. Some punishment! Not only was she being moved away from Debbie Rickard, but she was being told to sit next to Sue. She wondered if Tish would be furious at being split up from Sue but, as she went back there with her books, she could tell that she didn't mind. Sue, after all, would still be next door to her, just across the gangway, and Judy Sharp was pleased to have Tish sitting next to her. Debbie was relieved to be getting someone new, and the whole form was delighted at the distraction, which looked as though it would delay the start of the English lesson by at least five minutes as desk lids banged and girls shuffled around.

Only Margot Lawrence felt rather put out. She was not particularly fond of Debbie Rickard, and she liked sitting at the back. On the other hand, she was supposed to put some glasses on to look at the blackboard, and often didn't bother. Now she would not need to. Miss Heath was quite aware of this factor.

When the form had settled down, Miss Heath produced a thick pile of exercise books from her bag, and that was when the second nice thing happened to Rebecca.

'I have marked your essays over the weekend and one of them is so outstanding that I have awarded it an A. Rebecca, will you come up here and read it out to the rest of the form, please.'

Rebecca had to go up to the front. She took her open exercise book from Miss Heath and then turned to face the form. Her hand shook very slightly and the exercise book wobbled.

'A Winter's Morning,' she began, very fast.

'Don't gabble, Rebecca.'

Rebecca took a deep breath, and then read her essay slowly and carefully. The whole form listened in attentive silence. Nobody chattered or passed notes. Then Rebecca went back to her seat.

'Congratulations!' said Sue, out of the corner of her mouth, and Rebecca stared at the bright red A written boldly at the bottom of her essay, still not quite able to believe it.

But this was only the beginning of a day of excitement for Rebecca.

After English, Miss Heath left the room and a general babble broke forth, desk lids banged and chairs scraped. Next lesson was French and Ma'm'selle Giscard could always be relied upon to be late.

Tish got up and warmed her rear on the radiator, which was under the window and just behind Rebecca's chair. She grabbed the back of Rebecca's blue jumper and gave a tug.

'Hey, you!'

'Yes?' Rebecca turned round to see her smiling, one black curl out of place and hanging over her left eye. 'What?'

'You've got something to hand in tonight now.'

'For the magazine –? But I haven't.'

'That essay.'

'But –' Rebecca tried not to look too excited, 'is that allowed? I mean it was homework, not written for the magazine at all.'

'Of course it's allowed! You can submit anything you want. Copy it out on decent paper and have it ready by seven – okay?'

Tish shot back into her chair as Ma'm'selle entered the room, and the conversation came to an abrupt end.

'*Bon jour.*'

'*Bon jour*, Ma'm'selle.'

Rebecca found it hard to concentrate on lessons that day. She consulted the timetable at the front of her rough book and saw that the only prep for Monday evening was Geography. She hoped it would not be something long and arduous. She had to copy out her essay for Tish in her best handwriting by seven o'clock, and that was more important than anything else!

To her relief they were required only to draw some

common ordnance survey map signs and learn them. Rebecca knew them already, as they had done this work at her previous school.

She stayed on in the form room after the last lesson and drew the signs in her Geography exercise book quickly, finishing just before the tea bell went. She raced off and washed her hands and got to the dining hall in good time. Sardines on toast, good! Lots of fruit and stuff to follow, ginger cake and plenty of tea to drink.

'Where can I get some decent paper, Elf?' she asked. She had settled down more or less permanently at the opposite end of the table from Tish and Co., next to Sally Elphinstone, whom she liked. 'Somebody said there's a stationery room in old school.'

'Tiny little room next to the library,' said Elf, a second helping of ginger cake halfway to her mouth. 'There'll be a prefect on duty there after tea, and you have to sign for everything.'

It was Elizabeth Exton who was on duty. Just the sight of the tall, hawk-faced Sixth Former made Rebecca feel nervous.

'I want some sheets of best paper, please.'

'What do you mean, some? Be precise.'

'Four sheets, please.'

'Here you are.' The mighty Editor of the school magazine doled out the paper, wrote something in a ledger and handed Rebecca a pen. 'Sign here.'

Rebecca took the paper, signed for it, and escaped. Having already collected her English exercise book and yellow pencil case from the form room, she went straight into the library. She sat down and copied out her essay, neatly and carefully, in the best italic handwriting that she reserved for important occasions.

She then designed a title page on which were written the words: *A Winter's Morning by Rebecca Mason Form II Alpha*. She enclosed the words in a square box, carefully ruled, and then drew a little snowman underneath.

Just after seven o'clock she went to deliver the essay to Tish, who was sitting at the corner table in the Second Year Common Room, with her wire tray waiting. There were two First Years ahead of her, shyly depositing their contributions in the tray. Tish, in fact, was in the middle of sifting through the pile of contributions that had already been handed in at the magazine meeting the previous Wednesday, making still more notes.

But she looked up and caught Rebecca's eye. 'Well done,' she said, looking at the essay. 'I like the snowman. Just stick it in the tray with the other things.'

Rebecca went out quickly, trying hard not to show any sign of emotion. What were the other contributions like? How stiff was the competition? She would have to wait until Wednesday evening to find out.

Later, she made her cocoa and ate her biscuits alone. She wished she had a special friend, but not for a moment did she regret breaking up with Debbie Rickard. The terrible homesickness of the previous evening did not return; it had been an exciting day and now – although she hardly dare admit it – she was bubbling with hope. She wanted to write to her parents, but she must wait until after the second magazine meeting on Wednesday evening. Supposing, just supposing, she had some good news for them?

On Wednesday evening every chair was taken in the Second Year Common Room and Rebecca stood at the back with some First Years.

'Down to business,' said Tish briskly. She took a folder out of her bag and held it up. 'I've short listed six items and all of them are good enough to appear in this term's school magazine. But it's the Golden Jubilee edition and it's going to be very crowded, so I propose we send through four. That will be decided by vote. The best one will have a gold star put on it, as you know.'

Rebecca was very tense. She could not see all the items in the folder. Was her essay amongst them?

'First,' Tish held up a pen and ink drawing of the little church that stood in the school grounds, and Rebecca heard the fair-haired First Year standing beside her give a quick gasp of pleasure. 'Only one piece of artwork from the First Years, but it's outstanding. You can all recognize it, and it was done by Susannah Skelhorn over the weekend. I'm going to pass it round, but please be very careful not to mark it.'

She pulled another piece of artwork from the folder.

'Also we have this drawing by Verity Williams, Form II Beta, and I want you all to look at that closely, as well.'

Carefully the drawings were passed round the room and Tish took some sheets of paper from the folder. Rebecca thought she recognized her essay, but for a moment she could not be sure.

'Now the written contributions. I shall read them out, and then I shall pass them round as well. There are two poems, by Hilda Watkins and Judy Sharp, and two essays, by Jenny Brook-Hayes and Rebecca Mason.'

Rebecca felt slightly dizzy. The suspense was unbearable. In a blur she heard Tish read through the items, slowly and carefully. It seemed to take an age and although she could hear the words clearly, they refused to register on her brain, even the words of her own essay.

There was another long delay as the written work was passed round, so that girls who were undecided how to vote could read things through to themselves. During this period there was a lot of whispering and rustling of paper. At last Tish thumped on the table.

'I think you've all seen enough now,' she said. 'We'll have the vote. For the benefit of new girls, you are only allowed to vote for *one* item – the one you like best – and the six girls concerned are not allowed to vote at all. Okay? Let's start.'

She went through each item in turn. Hands were raised, votes were counted and written down. The first four items did not receive many votes, and Rebecca began to feel excited, even hopeful.

'Fifth, the drawing of St Mary's Church by Susannah Skelhorn.'

It seemed to Rebecca that a forest of hands shot up.

'. . . seven . . . eight . . . nine. Nine votes.'

She felt a huge lump coming into her throat. How silly of her to imagine that her essay might get the gold star! Would it even be selected to go through at all?

'Last, "A Winter's Morning" by Rebecca Mason.'

Rebecca closed her eyes. She heard Tish's voice.

'. . . seven . . . eight . . . nine . . . ten . . . eleven. Eleven votes.'

She opened her eyes again. Girls were turning round and looking at her, smiling and clapping.

Susannah Skelhorn, who was standing right beside her, said shyly, 'Congratulations. You deserved to win.'

Rebecca felt weak at the knees. She had no idea that there were so many girls in the room – that there were still eleven votes left for her! Her essay had been voted best, it would get the gold star!

Tish announced which four items would go through and the meeting broke up. Only one person looked really sour – Roberta Jones, who once again had failed to get anything short-listed for the school magazine. Debbie Rickard came up to Rebecca.

'Congratulations,' she said, but her smile was forced.

When Rebecca went up to the table, Tish was actually in the act of sticking a large gold star on the front of the essay, just above the snowman's head. A small crowd gathered round.

'Does this mean –' began Rebecca. Her voice faltered. She had meant to walk out with quiet dignity, but she *had* to be sure. 'Does the gold star mean that it'll definitely go in *The Trebizon Journal*?'

'Of course,' said Tish, and she gave Rebecca a dazzling smile. 'And I'm taking the stuff straight to Elizabeth Exton now. Well done, Bec, I knew you would win.'

NINE

THE MAGAZINE COMES OUT

Rebecca went out into the grounds. The sun was sinking low and a game of hockey was just finishing on school pitch. The birds were twittering and as she came within sight of Parkinson, the big Victorian house where the Upper Sixth boarded, she darted into some trees and kept watch.

Sure enough, Ishbel Anderson came hurrying along five minutes later, entered the garden of Parkinson House by the side gate and went across and rang the bell, her folder under her arm. After a few moments, the door opened and somebody let her in.

Rebecca came out of her hiding place. Her essay was being delivered to the Editor of the school magazine. She had seen so, with her own eyes. It was all real! She raced away, knowing that if by any chance Tish should catch sight of her gawping at Parkinson House, she would think her absolutely mad.

'It's twenty minutes till cocoa time!' thought Rebecca, running exhilarated as the breeze blew through her fair hair. 'I'll run down to the beach and look at the waves.'

In her study, Elizabeth Exton was pacing up and down. It

was a very large room, with a long mahogany table under the windows, and was not only Elizabeth's study but also the editorial office of *The Trebizon Journal*. There were four chairs set round the table which was piled high with papers and pieces of artwork. There had been a meeting of the Editorial Committee that evening. The Editor of the school magazine was always allocated this beautiful study as a matter of course. Last year its occupant had been Mary Green, who was now beginning an exciting career on a national newspaper.

Mary Green was very much in Elizabeth Exton's thoughts. She knew that Mary had got her start as a direct result of her work on *The Trebizon Journal*, and Elizabeth had similar ambitions. Although Freddie Exton had many contacts in the world of commerce, he had few in newspapers or magazines, a field Elizabeth badly wanted to enter when she left school.

Elizabeth had been told that she was unlikely to get to University, and she had decided to devote all her talents this year to the editorship of the school magazine. She felt sure that if she could produce three dazzling issues of the famous *Journal*, it would make a big impression on a future employer. This first issue, to mark the magazine's Golden Jubilee, must be the most dazzling of all.

Elizabeth felt very confident at the way things were going. What she planned to do with this issue was daring – ambitious – people were going to be very impressed! The meeting with the Editorial Committee this evening had been nerve-racking: especially that long argument with Audrey, trust Audrey to be difficult. The trouble was that she had wanted to be Editor herself! For a time, Elizabeth had had visions of her triumph slipping through her fingers, and all her hard work in the holidays going for nothing. But she had won the day! She had made the Committee see reason, and won them round completely to her way of thinking. Emma had been a great ally.

Now Elizabeth was convinced that this term's issue of *The Trebizon Journal* was going to put everything that had gone before in the shade. It would make Mary Green's efforts look dull and pedestrian by comparison. It was all very satisfying.

Only in one way did Mary Green have the edge, and it was this that was causing Elizabeth to pace up and down the floor. She was having a tremendous struggle with her conscience. By long tradition, the last page of *The Journal* always carried a personal contribution from the Editor herself. It could be prose or poetry or artwork, anything for which the Editor had a talent. Mary's special contribution had always been a crossword puzzle, with the clues written in verse, and they had won great acclaim. Elizabeth could produce nothing as good as that.

The last page of the magazine was still a yawning blank and, the more she thought about it, the more convinced Elizabeth became that there was only one way to solve the problem. But it would mean going against her conscience, and Elizabeth didn't like doing that.

'Who's that?' she asked, jumpily, as someone tapped on the door.

'Ishbel Anderson.'

'Come in.'

Elizabeth stared blankly for a moment as Tish walked in with her folder. What was a Junior coming to see her for?

'I've got Juniper's contribution, in this folder,' said Tish. 'Would you like to see them?' she asked eagerly. 'I got cracking quickly, because of what you said –'

'Just put the folder on the table,' said Elizabeth. 'I'm very busy right now. I'll look at them later.'

Tish placed the folder on the table, disappointed, as Elizabeth dismissed her.

'Thank you, Ishbel.'

As she left the room, Tish said, 'They're very good this term. They really are.'

'Yes, yes,' said Elizabeth abstractedly, 'I'm sure they are. Well done.'

After Tish had gone, Elizabeth walked over to the long mahogany table. She picked up the folder and then, restlessly, put it down again.

'House contributions,' she mused. 'More problems.'

She snapped her finger and thumb together and walked over to her portable typewriter, which was on a side table. She sat down and fed in a sheet of paper.

'About time I had a notice given out,' she thought. 'Forgotten all about it. So much to think about.'

She carefully typed a notice to be given out at Assembly the next day.

Sitting in the sand dunes, Rebecca watched the waves breaking on the shore of Trebizon Bay. The distant sea was stained red by the setting sun, and a solitary fishing boat bobbed upon it in dark silhouette. Rebecca felt happy and at peace. At last she could write to her parents, because she had something really good to tell them. Not tonight; it was almost cocoa time. Tomorrow. In the meantime, she composed the letter in her head.

Miss Welbeck read Elizabeth's notice at Assembly on Thursday morning.

'All contributions to *The Trebizon Journal* must be handed

79

to Elizabeth Exton by this weekend,' announced the Principal. 'It goes to the printers next week, a fortnight early, because for the first time it is carrying some colour pages to mark its Golden Jubilee.'

Rebecca could tell from the groans and whispers that some of the Magazine Officers were not going to have their House contributions ready in time. She caught Tish's eye. Tish was smiling and giving the thumbs-up sign. Elizabeth had certainly sprung her announcement at short notice. How sharp of Tish, thought Rebecca, to have found out in advance. At least Juniper House was going to be represented in *The Journal* – represented by her, Rebecca Mason! She still found that an amazing thought.

'Here is a further announcement,' said Miss Welbeck. '*The Journal* will be at the special price of £2.25 pence this term, and all copies must be ordered in advance. It can be posted direct to families and friends, and order forms are now available from the School Secretary. They must be completed and handed in by the end of the month.'

Miss Welbeck looked up from the typewritten sheet and added a comment of her own. 'Remember, you can pay for your copies out of pocket money, but if you are ordering more copies than you can pay for, you must write and ask for your parents' permission in advance, as they will be getting the bills!'

Subdued laughter echoed around the hall and Miss Welbeck passed on to other notices. Rebecca hardly took them in; she was doing a swift calculation. Her parents were in Saudi Arabia now. She had some airmail forms in her bedside locker. If she wrote to them in the dinner hour, and caught today's post, they could get the letter and send a reply by airmail by the end of the month – easily.

Rebecca wanted the magazine to go to at least ten people. Not just her parents, but her favourite uncles and aunts, and both her grandmothers would want a copy – and so would her friends in London, Claire and Amanda. It was such an honour getting into *The Trebizon Journal*! She had a whole mental list of people who would feel proud of her and want to have a copy to keep. But all those copies were going to cost her father a fortune!

On second thoughts, she would ask her father to pay for just four copies – his and Mum's, the two grandmothers' and one for Great Aunt Ivy, who definitely couldn't afford to buy one herself. Uncle Bill, and Godmother Joan, and Claire and Amanda and the rest she would write to herself and ask them to send through the money to her if they wanted one. Good, that was settled.

Rebecca dashed off the letter to her mother and father in the dinner hour, sealed up the airmail form and ran and dropped it in the school post box in the main entrance hall of old building. She tried to picture her parents' faces as they opened it and read it through. For a moment she felt an ache, missing them.

She wrote all the other letters the same evening, as soon as she had finished her French prep. She wrote to Claire and Amanda jointly and begged them for news; in return she told them about Trebizon and, in ironic tones, about the disastrous Debbie Rickard.

Not for a moment did Rebecca regret breaking up with Debbie, even though it meant she had no special friend to go around with at Trebizon. She would make her way as best she could, and try and get the most out of life at her new school, and perhaps friendships would follow. At least she was beginning to make her mark.

The following weeks were a little lonely at times, but one

thing made them less so. Her services were in demand in connection with *The Juniper Journal*.

It had been decided to bring out the House publication once a week, and an editorial committee of three had been elected. This comprised Tish Anderson and Mara Leonodis from the Second Year and Susannah Skelhorn from the First Year. Mara and Susannah were assistant editors, collecting in news items and other contributions from girls in their year, and Tish was Editor-in-chief, laying out the two pages and then typing the stencils. It was decided to produce *The Journal* on a single sheet of duplicating paper, using front and back. This would keep the cost down to five pence.

Everyone agreed that it was better to produce something cheap and simple once a week, full of up-to-date news, than a more ambitious publication that could only come out perhaps once a month.

The excitement in Juniper House as the first issue was being prepared was infectious, and a steady stream of contributions came in, some of them quite silly. It had been decided to make Sundays the press day for *The Journal*, as that was a day when Tish had plenty of free time to type out the stencils and run them off on the duplicator in the evening. *The Journal* would then be on sale every Monday morning.

On the Saturday night before the first press day, Tish was sitting having cocoa with Sue Murdoch in the Common Room.

'We've got stacks of news items,' she said. 'I mean Joss is announcing the Under-14 hockey team for a start. That's the lead story. We've also got a piece about the four items we've submitted to *The Trebizon* this term. That's a bit stale, but there are still some people who don't know.

Also one of the First Years has come up with a gem of a story . . .'

She lapsed into silence.

'What's the problem then?' asked Sue.

'The balance seems wrong. We haven't got what they call feature material – quizzes, crosswords, anything like that.'

At that moment the door opened and Rebecca and Sally Elphinstone came into the Common Room with cocoa and biscuits.

'You'd better have my biscuits, Rebecca,' said the plump girl mournfully. 'I just get fatter and fatter. It's just not fair, I mean look at you. You eat like a horse and you're skinny.'

'I burn it all up,' said Rebecca, taking the biscuits. 'You burn your food slowly, Elf, that's all. You'd have been the envy of all your friends if you'd lived in the Stone Age, when food was short. I mean they tried to be fat then. They really envied people who had an efficient system like yours, which could create energy from next to nothing.'

Sally snorted, but Tish's face lit up. 'Hey, that's interesting, Rebecca,' she said. 'Know any more useless facts like that?'

'She knows plenty,' giggled Sue, speaking from experience of sitting next to Rebecca in class. 'She's always churning them out. Tell Tish that one about lichen and pure air, Rebecca. Hey – I know what you're thinking, Tish!'

'What's going on?' asked Rebecca with a smile. It was true that she had a mind that stored up off-beat information; her father often teased her about it. 'Going to write a book?'

'No, you are!' said Tish. 'At least not a book. A regular piece for *The Juniper Journal* called "Did you know –? by Rebecca Mason"! Hmm? I'm serious. I've just thought of it. How about it?'

'Fine!' said Rebecca, trying to hide her delight.

'Good. Then write out three useless facts for me by tomorrow dinner hour, the weirder the better. Our first issue goes to press tomorrow afternoon, as if you didn't know.'

So Rebecca became a regular contributor to *The Juniper Journal*; she also helped to work the duplicator sometimes on a Sunday evening and was one of a team of girls selling copies around the school at five pence each.

The news-letter came in for a lot of praise, especially from Miss Morgan, their House Mistress. She herself undertook to sell two dozen copies a week in the Staff Room. It was all good fun.

But for Rebecca the high point of the next few weeks was the post. There was a long letter from her parents in Saudi Arabia, full of all their news, and scarcely concealing their happiness that she had made a good start at Trebizon School. They were immensely proud that her essay was going to appear in the school magazine and her father asked her to order eight copies, instead of the four she had suggested.

The letters from her Godmother Joan, her Uncle Bill and her Uncle David were lovely – they all wanted copies of the magazine and sent postal orders, with some extra spending money thrown in. Claire and Amanda each wrote a super letter, in the same envelope, and asked her to order an extra copy – for Mr Goodfellow, the Headmaster at her old school in London.

Rebecca was very excited, counting the days till half-term. The long-awaited Golden Jubilee edition of *The Trebizon Journal* was expected to arrive at the school from the printers' sometime over the half-term holiday. Rebecca was spending half-term with her grandmother in

Gloucestershire, and the magazines would be there, at the school, when she got back.

All through the half-term holiday at her grandmother's she felt a pleasurable sense of anticipation.

'You're sure your father's paid for my copy?' asked her grandmother anxiously. 'I'm well able to pay for it, you know, Becky. I certainly don't want you paying for it out of your pocket money.'

'Stop worrying, Gran,' laughed Rebecca. 'It's all ordered, and paid for, by Dad. I only wish it could have arrived from the printers in time for me to bring it with me. But it'll be posted to you in a few days, direct from school.'

Later, reading through the first three stencilled issues of *The Juniper Journal*, her grandmother said, 'And why aren't you in the hockey team, my girl?'

Rebecca was quite startled by the pang she felt. 'I'm – I'm just not,' she said.

She thought ruefully of her ambitions at the start of the term. She was beginning to like hockey a lot now, and knew that she was playing reasonably well, although she had still not been given a chance to play in a forward position. There were too many good forwards around for that.

She felt quite envious of the girls who were in the Under-14 team, going off in a mini-bus on Saturday afternoons to play matches against other schools. She still had no inkling that the game she had been asked to join during her first week at Trebizon had in fact been a trial game, and that Joss Vining had assumed that her interest was nil.

'You can't get in everything at a school like Trebizon, Gran,' said Rebecca. She smiled. 'At least I'm going to be in the school magazine, and that's something, isn't it!'

But Rebecca was wrong.

She learnt the awful news as soon as she got back to

school after the half-term holiday. She was late back because of the awkward journey from Gloucestershire, and went straight up to the dormitory with her denim bag to unpack her weekend things.

Tish was waiting for her there, holding a copy of the magazine. It was fresh from the printers and had a lovely gold cover. Rebecca had eyes for nothing else. She did not see that Tish's face was white with rage.

TEN

TISH DECLARES WAR

'You weren't on the London train,' said Tish.

'I haven't been to London,' said Rebecca. She was staring at the magazine, mesmerized. It looked beautiful! 'I've been to my grandmother's and that meant a bus that went halfway round England –'

'I've been waiting for you!'

'Miss Morgan knew I'd be late,' said Rebecca. What on earth was Tish so angry about, so very, very angry? 'The magazine's arrived from the printers' then? It really looks something –'

She reached out her hand eagerly. She *had* to see.

To her surprise Tish took a step backwards and put the magazine behind her back. She had difficulty in speaking.

'It's not in there. Your essay's not in.'

'Not in?' said Rebecca, dully.

'*Nothing's* in. Nothing from Juniper, almost nothing from any of the other Houses, a few Sixth Form things and *that's all*.'

'But – it's quite thick – there must be a lot of stuff in it – are you sure?'

'Of course I'm sure!' Tish produced the magazine and leafed over the pages in her hands. Rebecca caught a glimpse of beautifully laid out pages, some of them in full colour, thick and glossy. She recognized the exquisite bird pictures that Elizabeth had been carrying in her big black bag on the train, the very first time she had ever met her. 'It's thick all right and there's a lot of stuff in it, just nothing to do with Trebizon School, that's all!'

All Tish's pent up disgust poured out. 'It's full of big names, Rebeck. Famous writers, famous artists – okay, one or two of them old girls of the school, but not all of them, by any means. Elizabeth Exton's been having a ball! That's how she spent the summer holidays, dashing around meeting famous people, asking them to do things for the Golden Jubilee issue, making herself out to be someone really important. Here, take a look.'

Rebecca turned away.

'No thanks, Tish. I – I don't think I can bear to.'

'All right. But I'll just read what she says at the beginning, so you can have a really good vomit. Listen:

> It is a great honour and privilege to me to present this, our Golden Jubilee issue of *The Trebizon Journal*, marking its fifty years of continuous and unbroken production. This term contributions from the school were not quite up to the usual high standard, but no matter. The editorial committee and I decided to break with tradition and invite in outside contributors; how proud and honoured we are that such famous and illustrious names have agreed to grace our pages, a fitting birthday tribute to our famous *Journal*. Elizabeth Exton. Editor.

Rebecca sat down on the edge of her bed, feeling weepy.

'I've got friends and relations who've ordered it,' she said dismally. 'They'll all be getting it. Do I feel a fool. I just didn't think that my essay wasn't up to standard for the magazine, after –'

'It was up to standard!' snapped Tish. 'So was everything else, I expect – except a lot of stuff went in too late. Don't you see, that's just hot air? Elizabeth didn't *want* anything from the school! She'd got everything she needed before term even started – she had it on the train, remember? Talked about meeting super people.'

'Yes,' nodded Rebecca. 'I remember.'

'Being made Editor just went to her head. She raced around seeing all these big names in the holidays and getting them to do things. After that the committee hardly had any choice but to agree with her that they should be published in the magazine. I mean to say,' just for a moment a weaker version of Tish's usual grin appeared, 'imagine sending out a rejection slip to Nadine Rossiter.' The famous novelist had contributed a short story to *The Trebizon Journal*.

'Yes, imagine.' Rebecca managed to raise a smile, but she felt very depressed. 'All the same, I guess the stuff from the school really wasn't up to standard. They could have found room for it, if it had been. Even added a couple of extra pages.'

'Rubbish!' said Tish. 'Elizabeth just didn't want to find room for it. She didn't want anything that might spoil her grown-up looking magazine. I expect she's angling to get a good job somewhere on the strength of this,' she added darkly.

Silently, Rebecca unpacked her things. She was beginning to feel worse and worse; utterly humiliated. Tish was pacing up and down the dormitory, deep in thought. When she finally stopped, Rebecca looked at her and said, 'There's nothing you can do about it, Tish.'

'Oh, isn't there?' muttered Tish, and went out.

Brave words, thought Rebecca. As if there were anything Tish could possibly do. As if a mere Second Year could challenge the mighty Sixth Former who was Editor of the school magazine! After all, she *was* the Editor, and her decision was final. She said the school contributions weren't up to standard, and she should know best.

The more Rebecca thought about it, the more convinced she became that she had been conceited and overconfident about her essay. If it were a school tradition always to publish something with a gold star on it, then the Editor and her committee must have thought it *very* bad to reject it.

She ate tea in silence, grateful for the sympathetic comments from the girls on her table, but relieved not to be expected to talk. She was dimly aware that Tish arrived for tea very late, looking puffed and dishevelled, and left the minute she had finished her pudding, without even waiting for a cup of tea.

After tea, Rebecca didn't quite know what to do with herself. At a time like this she missed very much not having a special friend, someone to whom she could pour out her feelings. She felt such a failure! She would have liked Tish to talk to her again: somehow she did make it sound as though it was not a question of the essay being rubbish.

Rebecca went over to old school, carefully avoiding the Office where she knew that her personal copy of *The Trebizon Journal*, ordered so eagerly a month ago, was waiting to be collected. She didn't want to collect it – not ever! She wondered if there were any way she could stop all the other copies being posted off that she had ordered and paid for. There probably wasn't.

She borrowed a book from the library and went back across the quadrangle gardens to Juniper, having decided to find a quiet corner in the Second Year Common Room for the evening. There were too many people reading *The Trebizon Journal* in the library for her liking.

But as soon as she peered through the open door of the Common Room, she saw what looked like a forest of gold-covered Journals, glinting and shining in the light of the reading lamps, as though to mock her. Every seat was taken, every space on the rugs was taken, and there were even girls perched on the tables. It appeared to Rebecca's jaundiced eye that every single one of them was reading the school magazine, hot from the press.

'I think it's brilliant,' she heard Roberta Jones say smugly. 'Trust someone like Elizabeth Exton to do things in style. I'm not at all put out now that my poems weren't chosen to go forward.'

'Tish Anderson's like a bear with a sore head.' That was Debbie Rickard's voice, and there was a definite snigger in it. 'Her stuff's been rejected. The Editor's *dared* to question her judgement –!'

Rebecca didn't want to hear any more, and didn't want to be seen, either. She remembered how Debbie had come up and congratulated her, after the second magazine meeting. The hypocrite!

Where to go and read her book? Rebecca remembered the form room. There was no prep tonight and so it was deserted. She sat at her desk and read until a bell began to ring. She saw by the clock that it was bedtime, so she lifted the lid of her desk to put the library book inside.

'Who's been through my desk?' she wondered. 'What a mess.'

She decided to give cocoa a miss, and went straight to

bed. Tish and Sue were easily last in the dormitory, rushing in just before lights out.

'What have you two been up to?' asked someone.

'You'll see in the morning.'

'Sssh!'

'Shut up.'

'Have a biscuit, Tish.'

'Shut *up*, you lot!'

It took Rebecca a long time to get to sleep that night. She felt that she had only slept for a couple of hours when somebody drew the curtain behind her bed and shook her awake. It was Tish, already up and dressed.

'Here's your English exercise book, Rebecca,' she said, slamming it down on the locker. 'I borrowed it from your desk yesterday.'

'Whatever for?' asked Rebecca rubbing her eyes.

She stared at Tish, who seemed to be in a much better mood this morning. She seemed almost cheerful, and there was a strange light in her eyes. Rebecca also saw that she was holding some duplicated sheets in her hand.

'I needed to copy something out on to a stencil,' said Tish airily. 'Here you are, you may as well be the first to have one *J.J.* – special issue – free of charge, hot off the press last night. Five of us are off to disseminate it around the school now.' Bye. See you at breakfast!'

Rebecca found herself sitting up in bed, the stencilled sheet in her hands. Tish had gone. So had Sue. So had Margot Lawrence, Sally Elphinstone and Mara Leonodis. Joanna Thompson and Jenny Brook-Hayes were still fast asleep.

She stared at the sheet that had been thrust into her hands and, slowly at first, began to read it:

JUNIPER JOURNAL – Special Free Issue

We challenge The Trebizon Journal, it said. *Elizabeth Exton should resign. She's not fit to be Editor.*

Rebecca gasped and started to read much, much more quickly. Key phrases leapt out of the page at her.

For fifty years The Journal has been written by the school ... for the school ... not by outsiders ... the Editor has no right to cast a slur on the school contributions ... some Magazine Officers were not given time ... As far as Juniper House goes, the slur is unfounded ... We can prove it ...

We throw open our editorial columns to all work that has been rejected by Elizabeth Exton. We will publish it for you! But first we start with Juniper's best –

The next line of type danced in front of Rebecca's eyes.

A WINTER'S MORNING – by REBECCA MASON, FORM II ALPHA

In growing excitement she read her own essay, printed out in full, right down to the bottom of the page and over on to the back. Tish had copied it word for word from her English exercise book.

At the bottom of the back page came a final exhortation:

Don't forget – send your rejected material to The J.J. We will print it and prove that the remark in the official school magazine is a slur on us all. This issue published by Ishbel Anderson – Magazine Officer – Juniper House.

Rebecca sank back weakly against her pillow. It was unbelievable. Tish had really done it. She had challenged no less mighty a person than Elizabeth Exton. Rebecca felt admiration for her courage, but it was mixed with dread.

What would happen to Ishbel Anderson now?

ELEVEN

REBECCA SEES A 'GHOST'

Rebecca got washed and dressed and kept out of everybody's way until breakfast time. She went and sat down by the lake, watched the ducks bobbing in and out of the reeds, and read the stencilled news-sheet over and over again.

She was excited to see her essay in print and to know that the whole school would be reading it. At the same time she was ashamed of feeling excited. What an incredible thing for Tish to do. Clearly there were others backing her up, people like Sue and Margot and dear old Elf. But the full wrath of those in authority would surely fall on Tish's head, and hers alone.

A group of Fourth Years went by, on their way to breakfast from their boarding house in the school grounds. They were crowding round the stencilled sheet as they walked along.

'I agree with every word she says!'

'So do I.'

'Suky Morris did a marvellous drawing and it should have gone in. Elizabeth Exton's just a big show-off.'

95

'But what's she going to do when she reads this? That's what I want to know . . .'

Their voices faded off into the distance. Rebecca got to her feet. She couldn't put off going to dining hall any longer, and besides, she wanted breakfast badly. It was an hour since Tish had shaken her awake. In that hour, Tish and Co. had certainly moved fast: the special issue of *The J.J.* had already been delivered to the boarding houses. People were already reading it.

Rebecca could tell, as soon as she entered the dining hall, that the news had travelled like wildfire. The stencilled sheets were in evidence everywhere and there was a tremendous buzz of talking. Tish, trying to sit down to have her breakfast, was involved in a quarrel with someone – it looked as though it might turn into a physical fight. And as Rebecca walked in, a group of First Years on the table nearest the door clapped her.

'Get your hands off me, Margaret Exton!' Tish was saying, as Rebecca approached. A tall girl with bony features, was gripping Tish's arm tightly and Tish was trying to tear her hand away. 'Get lost!'

Rebecca remembered that Elizabeth Exton had a younger sister in the Third Year. This must be her – white with fury, too.

'You'll pay for this, Tish Anderson,' she said threateningly.

'Go and sit at your proper table, Margaret,' said a prefect.

Margaret Exton walked across the hall to her table, where a group of Third Years banged their knives and forks and cheered her.

Miss Gates, the mistress on duty, blew a whistle loudly.

'Silence!' she said. 'Everyone will eat breakfast in silence!'

And so they did. Immediately afterwards, Rebecca approached Tish before she could leave the dining hall.

'Tish!'

'Are you angry, Rebecca?'

'No, I'm just scared for your sake.'

'I'm not scared. I just had to do something – and I feel great to have got it all off my chest. Sorry it happens to be your essay that's involved. Means your name's dragged into the whole thing.'

'I don't mind *that* at all!' said Rebecca, her eyes shining now. 'You've certainly got a lot of faith in that essay! Not only you, but the others who've helped you. I'd just about lost faith in it. But now, seeing it in print . . .'

'Six different people have already told me they think it's marvellous,' said Tish. 'I mean, older girls. Even a Sixth Former.'

As if to prove the very point that Tish was making, two older girls walked over and clapped Rebecca on the back.

'Good stuff that.'

'Should have gone in.'

But another girl, Lady Edwina Burton who was in the Fifth Year, came up to them and said quite angrily, 'Don't encourage these little berks. They're big-headed enough already. Who do they think they are, anyway?'

'Hear, hear!' said somebody else.

Fortunately, at that moment the bell went for Assembly.

During the course of the day, Rebecca came to realize that the school was split right down the middle, taking sides in the quarrel between the puny *Juniper Journal* and the mighty *Trebizon Journal*.

A lot of girls agreed with Tish's views, and were quietly pleased that she had expressed them. But there were others who admired the beautiful, lavish magazine that Elizabeth

Exton and her committee had produced to mark the Golden Jubilee, and thought the whole thing was rudeness and cheek beyond belief.

As for Elizabeth Exton, there was no doubt in her mind whatsoever. As soon as a copy of the offending sheet fell into her hands, at the end of a morning break, she went directly to see Miss Morgan, House Mistress of Juniper.

'I think this insolent little rag should be banned,' she informed Miss Morgan. 'These girls aren't sensible enough to have the use of a duplicating machine. They should never be allowed to use it again. Especially that Anderson girl.'

Miss Morgan read the news-sheet from start to finish.

'I see,' she said at length. 'Thank you for drawing this to my attention, Elizabeth. Perhaps you could arrange for Ishbel to be extracted from old school and brought over here to my office at once.'

'Yes, Miss Morgan,' said Elizabeth, with some satisfaction.

In spite of her protests to Rebecca about not being scared, Tish was only human. Her knees began to knock when she found herself hauled out of the French lesson and deposited in Miss Morgan's office on the ground floor of Juniper House. The room was empty but she could see the stencilled sheet lying on the desk.

Some time later, Miss Morgan walked in, sat down and picked up the sheet, fixing Tish with a stern eye.

'You shouldn't have done this, Ishbel.'

'But it wasn't fair!'

'You do realize, don't you, that if it were not for the generosity of Elizabeth's father, there would be no magazine at all this term?'

'Yes, but that shouldn't come into it –'

'Of course not. Except it should make you doubly careful

before you insult and vilify somebody without any possible justification, somebody much higher up the school than you who has worked extremely hard, in full and proper consultation with her editorial committee –'

'But –'

'Don't argue with me, Ishbel. That fact, I have just checked. And as you know, anybody elected to the high office of Editor of *The Journal* has, with her editorial committee, final responsibility for it. It's not up to any of us, least of all some insignificant members of the Second Year, to question her judgement in such personal terms.

'Elizabeth has asked me to ban your journal. I am not going to ban it. Indeed, you're free to publish any material you wish that did not reach the necessary standard for this term's magazine. But first you'll publish a full apology and retraction for this –' She tapped the sheet lying on the table. 'Draft something out and bring it to my office this evening.'

She got up and showed Tish to the door.

'Ishbel, I'm surprised at you,' were Miss Morgan's last words.

'Tish!' shouted Sue, hanging out of the form room window and waving. French had just ended and four of them, including Rebecca, were crowding round the window that looked down on to the quadrangle gardens, far below. At last Tish had emerged from Juniper House. 'Tish!'

'She's coming back, but she's not looking up,' said Margot Lawrence apprehensively. 'I don't think she's even heard us.'

'She looks really miserable,' said Elf. 'She's come into the building now. I wonder what the punishment is?'

'Whatever it is, we share it with her,' said Margot. 'We were all in it together.'

'I'll share it, too,' volunteered Rebecca.

They rushed over as Tish entered the form room, her cheeks red and her grin noticeably absent. Debbie Rickard, sat in the front row, all ears, pretending to sort out her history books for the next lesson.

'What happened?'

'What is it – lines? Detention? What?'

'Nothing like that,' began Tish. She was very subdued. 'Gosh, did I get an earful from Miss Morgan! She's backing up Elizabeth Exton completely. Won't hear a word against her.'

Debbie Rickard glanced across the form room and caught the eye of Roberta Jones. They exchanged satisfied nods.

'Look out!' shouted Judy Sharp, who was keeping watch in the corridor. 'Maggy's coming!'

There was a mad scramble for desks and books as Miss Magg, the history mistress, entered the form room.

'No whispering, please,' she said sternly.

Sitting next to Sue at the back, Rebecca tried to concentrate as Miss Magg wrote some facts about Ancient Egypt on the blackboard. Out of the corner of her eye she saw Tish pass Sue a note, across the gangway between their desks. Sue opened it out and let Rebecca read it with her. It said:

Have to apologize to E.E. in the J.J. or else . . .

Sue wrote underneath:

And will we?

She passed it to Tish, who wrote something and passed it back:

Horrible decision. I don't know.

All Rebecca's thoughts were with Tish now. Poor Tish. No wonder she looked so unhappy! She respected Miss Morgan and was obviously shattered that she sided with Elizabeth. But what else could the House Mistress do?

reflected Rebecca. No Second Year could insult an important School Officer and be allowed to get away with it. In her heart, she had guessed it would come to something like this.

'The tomb, Rebecca!' said Miss Magg sharply. 'What did they put in the tomb?'

'The – the body, I suppose,' said Rebecca weakly. There was laughter. Maggy had been asking her a question and she hadn't even heard it.

'Oh, really? The body?'

The mistress's voice was heavy with sarcasm and from then on Rebecca had to pay close attention to the lesson. At last the bell went. Morning lessons had ended; in fifteen minutes it would be dinner time.

Tish and Co. immediately went into a huddle over by the window. Rebecca wondered if she could join them, but Sue signalled her away. They were discussing whether Tish should write the apology.

'Action committee, Rebecca,' mouthed Tish. 'Clear off. We're mixed up in it, especially me, but you're not. Not fair to involve you.'

Rebecca wandered downstairs, thinking she wouldn't mind being mixed up in it. The Secretary popped her head out of the School Office and called her name. She was holding *The Trebizon Journal*.

'You've forgotten to collect your magazine, Rebecca.'

Rebecca had no choice but to take it. After all, she had paid for it. And as she sat in the weak November sunshine outside the dining hall, waiting for the bell to go, curiosity got the better of her at last. Gingerly, she began to leaf through the pages.

She was looking at the last page when Tish found her. The dinner bell had gone, but Rebecca hadn't even heard it.

Tish was feeling extremely angry and upset at the idea of having to write a public apology to Elizabeth Exton, and so far nothing had been resolved. But she was not so upset that she couldn't see there was something wrong.

'Reading that?' she asked. Then, 'What's the matter with you? You look as though you've seen a ghost.'

'My poem!' said Rebecca, hoarsely, almost too shocked to speak. It really was like seeing a ghost. 'She didn't write it. *I* did.'

TWELVE

OUT OF THE FRYING PAN . . .

'Your poem?' asked Tish, bewildered. 'What on earth are you talking about, Rebecca? Who didn't write what?'

'Elizabeth Exton didn't write my poem!' blurted out Rebecca. 'I wrote it! She's made up a title for it – "Solitude" – that's all. I called it "All Alone", but it's *my* poem. I wrote it! And she's put *her* name at the bottom of it!'

'Are you serious?' Tish said.

The last stragglers were going into the dining hall now and shortly a prefect would close the big glass doors. But neither Rebecca nor Tish were conscious of that. Tish snatched the gold-covered *Trebizon Journal* out of Rebecca's hands.

'You mean here on the last page, the place that's always reserved for the Editor's own personal work –'

Tish was speaking in a tremendous rush. She was out-raged, but beneath the outrage there was a tinge of triumph and excitement in her voice.

'"Solitude",' she read out. Then, '"There's a certain slant of light, on winter afternoons. It falls through the trees, lies heavy on the . . ."'

'"Dunes."' Rebecca finished the line, automatically. She kept pushing a hand through her hair, wondering if she were dreaming the whole thing. 'That's exactly what I wrote – the whole thing. I don't believe she's altered a single word. It was the first day I arrived here. I was feeling really miserable. I went down to the bay, and sat in the dunes, and wrote it –'

'I remember!' said Tish. 'I looked for you. I was waiting for you when you came back and we were late for tea. And,' she ended triumphantly, 'you had biro on your face. You had to wash it off!'

She stared at the poem, in mounting excitement. 'Of course!' she said under her breath. 'I hadn't even read this, but now I have – it's not her at all, is it? It's much more you, Rebecca. How could she be so daft? Surely she knows she's going to be found out!' Tish grabbed Rebecca's arm. 'How did she get hold of it? Where was it? Have you kept a copy? Have you got your rough working out –?'

Rebecca just shook her head, the feeling of extreme unreality returning. That was what was so amazing about it all. 'I just wrote it on the beach,' she said dully. 'When I'd finished it, I felt a whole lot better. So I just ripped the page out of my notepad and put it in a litter basket.'

'What?' Tish's face fell. 'You didn't!'

Rebecca knew there was no need to reply. Tish believed her. She just shrugged her shoulders helplessly. And suddenly Tish saw the funny side of it.

'How ridiculous!' she laughed. She felt slightly hysterical. 'Do you mean to say Elizabeth Exton was so desperate to find something to pass off as her own work that she went poking around all the litter baskets in Trebizon Bay!'

'Looks like it!' Rebecca was beginning to feel hysterical herself. 'The latest craze – punk poetry!'

'It's a wonder she didn't print the words off an ice-cream

wrapper!' giggled Tish helplessly. 'Oh, Rebecca, this is all just too marvellous –'

'Marvellous?' said Rebecca, suddenly sober.

'Ishbel Anderson! Rebecca Mason! Come on – at once!'

The duty prefect had come over to close the doors and had seen the two of them still outside.

'Tish!' said Rebecca anxiously, as they hurried into the hall. 'Don't do anything silly. I know you believe me, but I don't think anybody else would. And there's not a hope of proving anything. You're in enough trouble already. I wish I hadn't told you. I'm not going to tell anybody else. I want to think it all over –'

'Yes, so do I,' said Tish suddenly.

'And you promise –?' began Rebecca. She was having to hurry to keep up with the dark-haired girl as they threaded their way through the crowded dining hall. 'You promise –?'

'I promise to do nothing silly this time,' said Tish.

As Rebecca and Tish sat down at opposite ends of the dinner table, Rebecca heaved a sigh of relief. Tish had given her promise not to do anything silly. Rebecca didn't want her getting into any more trouble on her account.

Maybe she, Rebecca, would have to summon up courage and confront the mighty Elizabeth Exton about the poem, but it would need some careful thought. Maybe she could have a meeting this evening with what Tish called her 'Action Committee', and see if *they* believed her. And if they did . . .

Maybe, maybe, maybe . . . All through the dinner hour Rebecca churned the problem round in her mind. She longed to talk it over with Tish. But Tish had gone off with Sue for a walk in the school grounds. Rebecca guessed that they would be talking over Tish's problem, whether or not to publish the apology to Elizabeth Exton in *The Juniper*

Journal. What would Sue advise? She felt deeply envious of their close friendship.

Rebecca also surmised that Tish would be telling Sue about her poem. Well, she didn't mind that. Would Sue believe it? As long as Tish didn't do anything reckless, that was the main thing! Rebecca felt fairly calm, because Tish had promised faithfully not to do anything silly. It never occurred to her that Tish had chosen her words with care. As far as Tish was concerned, what she had made up her mind to do was not silly at all – but perfectly sensible. And she certainly wasn't going to run the risk of Rebecca putting a stop to it.

It was a games afternoon, and Tish did not turn up. Even then, Rebecca suspected nothing. Sue told Miss Willis that Tish had a bad headache, and had gone to lie down in the sick room – and Rebecca believed it! She thought of the awful decision Tish had to make about the apology. That was enough to give anyone a bad headache.

After games, there was a whole free period before tea. Rebecca took a shower in the sports centre and planned to go and ask Matron how Tish was. But as she came out of the changing rooms, she heard a hubbub going on in the foyer where at least a dozen girls were crowding round the big notice-board.

'It's another special edition of *The J.J.*!'

'Tish Anderson's been pinning them up all over the school!'

'What does it say – here, let's have a look!'

'Is it true?'

'No, can't be!'

'She'll be rusticated now. That's for sure. She's mad!'

Rebecca walked slowly over to the notice-board, perspiration breaking out on the palms of her hands. She stood on tip-toe at the back of the crowd. There was a duplicated sheet pinned up but the stencil had obviously been made in a great hurry, because there were a lot of typing errors. However, what it had to say was clear and to the point:

JUNIPER JOURNAL – Special Issue No. 2

As the person mainly responsible for publishing Special Issue No. 1, I have been asked to retract and apologize to Elizabeth Exton. Before I will consider doing this, I must ask Elizabeth Exton to apologize to Rebecca Mason. In the Golden Jubilee edition of The Trebizon Journal, Elizabeth has published a poem called 'Solitude' as her own work. Below, I publish the poem under its real title, and under the name of the true author. Ishbel Anderson, Magazine Officer, Juniper House

Then came the title of the poem, and Rebecca's name: ALL ALONE by REBECCA MASON FORM II ALPHA, and then the poem in full.

Rebecca turned away, quickly. In the excitement, nobody had noticed her standing there. She hurried outside and into the grounds, and started walking. The trees were painted with the warm colours of autumn and leaves were falling. Her heart was beating very fast and she was gripped with exultation. And she had imagined Tish laid low with a headache!

She would never have dared to do something like this, but Tish certainly had! And now it had happened, Rebecca knew that it was right. The poem business justified every word Tish had put in the first Special Issue. Elizabeth Exton was *not* fit to be Editor of the school magazine. She *ought* to resign! And now the whole world would know it.

But Rebecca's exultant feelings were short-lived. Elizabeth Exton had also found a copy of the stencilled sheet, pinned on the notice-board in the entrance hall of Parkinson House. She took it down and went and made a strong cup of tea in the kitchen; she was glad that there was nobody else around as she gathered her wits together. How unlucky! What an awful bore! Her survival now depended on how ruthless she could be. It was them – or her. She imagined her father's anger if this should ever come to his ears, and she knew that she must stop at nothing.

Elizabeth marched straight across to see the Principal of Trebizon School, the stencilled sheet in her hand. As she entered the big study, she was surprised to find that Miss Welbeck already had copies of both Special Issues on her desk. They had been left with her, just before, by Miss Morgan.

'Come in, Elizabeth,' said Miss Welbeck, in calm tones. 'Miss Morgan has just been telling me about all this. I'd seen one of two of the early issues of their little House Journal and I must say I was quite impressed. Pity they have to spoil it with this sort of thing.'

The Principal of Trebizon School regarded her Sixth Formers as young adults which, indeed, they were. She trusted them completely and treated them as equals.

'I am very angry, Miss Welbeck, as you can well imagine.'

'I'm sure you are, Elizabeth. I shall see the culprit presently. I feel rather sorry for the little Mason girl, but I am very surprised at Ishbel Anderson's behaviour.'

'Quite,' said Elizabeth, pleased at the way things were going.

The Principal got up and walked to the window. A mist was coming down beyond the oak trees. The days were drawing in. She was feeling vexed and it would help to talk things over with Elizabeth.

'I'm afraid I myself encouraged Rebecca to have ambitions,' said Miss Welbeck ruefully. 'I imagine it was a great disappointment to her when her essay was not accepted for *The Trebizon*.' She glanced at Elizabeth. 'It is quite good, you know.'

'Indeed, yes. One of the few really good items this term,' lied Elizabeth. 'In a normal issue, it would have gone in. As a matter of fact, I had already decided to hold it over and use it in next term's *Trebizon*.'

'Good.' Miss Welbeck nodded her approval. 'The trouble is, the child is dying to make some sort of impression. I gather from Miss Morgan that she's something of a loner and has not made any special friends yet. She's completely unused to boarding school life, and her parents going abroad was no doubt a great shock to her . . .'

As Miss Welbeck continued to speak her thoughts aloud, Elizabeth listened demurely, nodding wisely at intervals.

'Clearly she admired your poem enormously, and has invented a little fantasy about it. She has pretended to Ishbel that she has written one just like it. Most disturbing really. As if –' the Principal turned away, looking out of the window across the park land. Elizabeth only just caught the next words. '– As if a girl of Rebecca's age would have met up with Emily Dickinson.'

Even as Elizabeth pondered over these last words and wondered what Miss Welbeck was talking about, the Principal turned and came back to her seat. With a heavy sigh, she sat down.

'No, it is Ishbel who has behaved outrageously. To have accepted this fantasy without question! I shall see Ishbel on her own. She will now have to make a double retraction and a double apology, instead of just the one that Miss Morgan called for. She will be the laughing stock of the school. So, unhappily, will Rebecca Mason, and I regard that as very unfortunate.'

Leaving the Principal's study, it was Elizabeth Exton who now felt exultant. She went back to her boarding house and made a fresh pot of tea in the kitchen, humming softly to herself. There was just one irritating little question that kept nagging at her mind.

When Audrey Maxwell came into the kitchen to get a biscuit, Elizabeth burst out, 'Audrey, have you ever met up with someone called Emily Dickinson?'

'You mean the poet?'

'Er – yes.'

'You must be off your rocker,' said Audrey. 'She's been dead for over a hundred years.'

Audrey went out nibbling the biscuit, thoughtfully. There was something very odd about the question Elizabeth had just asked her. It wasn't just her ignorance – Audrey was used to that. There was something particularly odd, but for the moment she couldn't quite put her finger on it.

THIRTEEN

...AND INTO THE FIRE

Tish spent only five minutes in the Principal's study. It was a close encounter of the bad kind.

'Come, come, Ishbel. You have made a silly accusation. You have spread it right round the school! And you have not one shred of evidence to back it up –'

'Then you haven't spoken to Elizabeth Exton?' said Tish. 'Please, Miss Welbeck, you should –'

'I have spoken to Elizabeth and she has reacted with a forbearance that would quite surprise you. You don't deserve it. I believe you have taken leave of your senses, Ishbel, to print this nonsense on your duplicator. You will go now and compose a full retraction and apology. After that has been printed you will never be allowed to use the machine again.'

'But I just *know* it's Rebecca's poem!' gasped Tish. 'I can't prove it, but I just believe her, that's all –'

'Stop this nonsense at once, please, Ishbel. Do as I tell you. Retract everything you have said in both issues of the news-sheet. Show the draft to Miss Morgan, as she asked you to this morning. That's all. You may go.'

Tish walked across to the door of the study, then stopped.

'And – and if I don't, Miss Welbeck?' she asked, in a very small voice.'

Miss Welbeck was picking up the internal telephone and dialling a number. She did not even look up as she replied.

'Then you will not be allowed to remain at Trebizon,' she said.

Tish went and stood outside, pressing her forehead against the wall for a few moments. In a blur, she could just hear Miss Welbeck speaking on the phone to Jacquinda Meredith, the Senior Prefect.

'Get some volunteers and see that every single copy is rounded up, please. Then make sure they are destroyed. What? You haven't seen it yet? You have missed nothing.'

Tish walked away, angry and tearful.

Later, Rebecca looked for her everywhere. She had been for a walk in the grounds and then raced back to Juniper. She had suddenly realized that there would be an almighty row about what Tish had done. And although Rebecca never doubted for a moment that Elizabeth Exton would confess, she wanted to be around when the whole thing blew up so that she could answer questions and back Tish up.

'She's with Miss Welbeck,' Sue Murdoch told her. Sue looked rather pale and tense. 'She's been there about fifteen minutes. I expect Elizabeth Exton's there, too. There'll be a big showdown going on.'

'Didn't – didn't Miss Welbeck want to see me, too?' asked Rebecca in concern. The storm broken already! She hated the idea of Tish seeing the whole thing through on her own. 'Was there a message?'

'Nope,' said Sue. 'She just wanted Tish.'

Rebecca raced over to old school. Girls advanced on her, some of them looking angry.

'You didn't really write that poem, did you?'

'What's Tish Anderson putting this sort of thing around for?'

But Rebecca dodged away from them. She had to know what was going on. At the foot of the main staircase she nearly collided with Pippa Fellowes-Walker, who was always friendly towards her.

'Pippa! Please, have you seen Tish? Is she still with the Head?'

'She came out a few minutes ago. She looked like death.'

Rebecca began to feel distinctly sick. Surely Elizabeth Exton had confessed? Surely Miss Welbeck couldn't be angry with Tish, when the truth was on her side? Had something gone wrong?

She searched for Tish in the old building, first in the form room and then the library. Then she went back to Juniper House. She pulled up short in the doorway. There was a crowd of girls outside the TV room, talking and banging on the closed door. Something very dramatic was going on. Suddenly, all together, they started to move away up the corridor, and Rebecca caught snatches of whispered conversation.

'Come on, the best thing we can do is leave Sue Murdoch in peace.'

'But she's locked herself in! Shouldn't we do something?'

'Of course not. She just wants to be left alone.'

'Who wouldn't? It's the most rotten thing that's ever happened.'

'It's all Rebecca Mason's fault!'

'You just shut up, Debbie Rickard!'

The moment they had gone upstairs, Rebecca ran forward and rattled the handle of the door to the TV room.

'Sue, it's me. Please let me in.'

She heard a muffled sob; then the catch inside the door was released and Sue opened it. Rebecca hardly recognized her; she had taken her spectacles off and her eyes were very red.

'What's happened? Where's Tish?'

'She's packed her things and now she's with Miss Morgan. She's asking Miss Morgan to ring her father to come and fetch her home. I expect Miss Morgan is trying to talk her round. But I know Tish. She's stubborn.'

Sue knelt on the floor and buried her face deep in the armchair. 'She's got to apologize to Elizabeth Exton or else leave the school. Well, Tish believes you wrote that poem and that's that. She'd rather be rusticated than apologize to that liar.'

'Sue!'

Rebecca sank down into the armchair. Her legs felt very weak and wobbly. So Elizabeth Exton had denied everything and Miss Welbeck believed her! It was Elizabeth's word against Rebecca's. The word of the mighty Editor of the school magazine against that of a pale and insignificant new girl. The chilling truth dawned on Rebecca at last.

'Miss Welbeck thinks I made the whole thing up!' she thought. 'She thinks I was just shooting a big line to Tish! She didn't even think it was worth calling me up to her study, to question me! I expect she feels sorry for me, and will give me a little talking-to sometime. It's Tish she's angry with, for believing me!'

Rebecca's head began to ache painfully.

'Sue,' she said numbly. 'You know I never wanted Tish to do anything like this. But to be honest, when I saw what she'd done, I was thrilled to bits. I just took it for granted that Elizabeth would own up. And then everyone would see that what Tish said about her not being fit to be Editor was true.'

'That's just how my mind worked,' said Sue. 'We talked about it at dinner break. I told her she was doing the right thing and that Elizabeth would be sure to own up –' She looked absolutely woebegone. '– but, she hasn't, and she never will. And Tish certainly won't apologize. So that's that. Tish is out.'

'But nobody's even talked to me yet!' cried Rebecca. She got up suddenly, and although the movement made her head throb, she rushed to the door. 'Doesn't anybody want to hear what I've got to say?'

She ran out of Juniper and on to the terrace. Small groups of girls were drifting about near the dining hall, waiting for the tea bell to go. But tea was the last thing on Rebecca's mind. She crossed the gardens and let herself into old school. The thought of going and knocking on the door of the Principal's study, completely uninvited, frightened her to death.

As she reached the top of the main staircase, she was just in time to see a tall figure entering Miss Welbeck's study. It was Elizabeth Exton. In that moment, fright left Rebecca and anger took over. She ran to the door before Elizabeth could close it.

'I'm coming in, too! I've a right to speak to Miss Welbeck, as well!'

'Wait outside, please, Rebecca,' came the Principal's calm voice. 'I thought you might turn up. But I'd like to speak to Elizabeth first.'

The door closed. Trembling, Rebecca sat down and waited. She wanted to yell and shout and rush in there and pull Elizabeth's hair. Somehow, she must control her feelings and wait until she was summoned.

FOURTEEN

THE MIGHTY FALLEN

Although Miss Welbeck had called out to Rebecca in a calm voice, she was less calm than she sounded. First of all, Miss Morgan had telephoned through to her from Juniper, and told her about Ishbel Anderson's stubborn and melodramatic behaviour. It seemed she had already packed her bags. The Principal had instructed the House Mistress on no account to telephone Ishbel's father, but to keep the girl in her office until she, Miss Welbeck, had had the opportunity of interviewing Rebecca Mason.

It was obvious that Ishbel was acting out of misguided loyalty to the new girl, and still believed her ridiculous story about the poem. Miss Welbeck decided that she must see Rebecca at once, and explain to her how serious the matter had now become. What had probably started as a silly piece of boasting on Rebecca's part had got completely out of hand. Rebecca must now admit the truth to Ishbel, and the sooner the better.

But before the Principal could arrange for Rebecca to be brought to her study, she had received an unexpected visitor in the shape of Audrey Maxwell. Audrey was someone whom Miss Welbeck held in high regard, and she was surprised to find her arriving without an appointment. She knew that it must be something important.

Earlier that afternoon, Audrey had been sitting in the comfortable little sitting room at Parkinson House, doing some private study, when Jacquinda Meredith had come in with a wad of papers. She had stuffed them in the fireplace and looked around for some matches.

'Lighting a fire before tea, Jackie?' Audrey had asked in surprise.

'The Head asked me to collect these up and burn them,' said the Senior Prefect. 'It's those Second Years again. They've really gone too far this time, sticking this up all round the school. I've heard that Tish Anderson's going to be rusticated.'

'Here, let's have a look,' said Audrey.

As soon as she had read the sheet that Jacquinda gave her, Audrey got to her feet, looking agitated. Now she remembered! She had felt there was something wrong when Elizabeth Exton had known nothing about Emily Dickinson – at last, she had pinpointed the reason!

'Did you ever read such rubbish?' Jacquinda was saying.

'I'm not sure it is rubbish,' said Audrey, keeping hold of the sheet. 'I'm going to see what Miss Heath thinks.'

Miss Heath was in the next room, giving two members of the Upper Sixth a tutorial in English Literature. It was on the advice of Miss Heath, who was of course Rebecca and Tish's form-mistress, that Audrey then went immediately across to old school and saw Miss Welbeck. As a direct result of Audrey's visit, Miss Welbeck had now summoned Elizabeth Exton to come and see her at once.

'Sit down, please Elizabeth.' The Principal fixed her gaze on her, and the Sixth Former returned it unflinchingly.

'When I saw you earlier I accepted without question that the poem "Solitude" was your own work. Can you, in fact, assure me that it is? Or are there any other factors that I ought to know about?'

'Of course it's my own work, Miss Welbeck.'

'Audrey Maxwell assures me that you know nothing about Emily Dickinson. If that is so, I find it very strange.'

Elizabeth took a deep breath. Miss Welbeck's reference to someone called Emily Dickinson earlier that afternoon had bothered her. It had bothered her still further to learn from Audrey Maxwell that Emily Dickinson had been a poet.

Although she was still baffled as to the significance of this person, Elizabeth had gone straight to the school library and read up about her. She was not going to be caught napping!

'I can't imagine why Audrey Maxwell should say that,' retorted Elizabeth. 'Of course I know about Emily Dickinson. She was an American poet who lived and died in the last century.'

Miss Welbeck made no reply.

Elizabeth was beginning to feel out of her depth. What was Miss Welbeck driving at? She turned to the attack. 'I'm surprised at Audrey if she's been saying things about me. Of course, it's common knowledge that she badly wanted to be Editor of *The Trebizon Journal* herself.'

'Yes,' Miss Welbeck got to her feet and walked over to the door. 'I daresay she did.' She opened the door. 'Rebecca, would you like to come in now, please?'

Rebecca was very overwrought. It had been agonizing, waiting outside. At last she was being summoned. She came into the panelled study, bursting to speak, and not quite sure where to begin.

'Miss Welbeck —'

'Sit down, please, Rebecca.' Miss Welbeck waved her to a chair, away from Elizabeth's. 'I can see that you have a lot of things to say to me, and you will have the chance to do so. But first, I want you to be very quiet until you are spoken to.'

Rebecca sat down, suddenly soothed by Miss Welbeck's presence. There was something so confident and reassuring about her, just as there had been the first time she had entered this study. Elizabeth Exton was looking tense and strained by comparison. Rebecca had the strange feeling that everything was going to be all right. The throbbing in her head began to subside.

'Elizabeth, let me ask you a question,' said the Principal. 'Let us take this first line of the poem: "There's a certain slant of light, on winter afternoons . . ." Now, how would you say it goes on from there?'

Elizabeth stared at the Principal. Surely she did not expect to catch her out as easily as that! Why, she knew the poem off by heart and back to front.

'"It falls through the trees, lies heavy on the dunes . . ."' began Elizabeth. Before she could get any further, Miss Welbeck signalled her to stop, with a sharp gesture.

'Thank you, Elizabeth.' She turned to Rebecca. 'And now your turn, Rebecca. "There's a certain slant of light, on winter afternoons . . ." How would you say the poem goes from there?'

Rebecca screwed up her eyes tightly for a moment, then said:

'". . . *That oppresses, like the weight of cathedral tunes.*
Heavenly hurt it gives us; we can find no scar,
But internal difference where the meanings are.
None may teach it anything . . ."'

'Good!' exclaimed Miss Welbeck, cutting Rebecca off in mid-sentence. 'I see you know your Emily Dickinson. Do you admire her poems?'

'I find them rather difficult,' Rebecca admitted, speaking shyly. 'But I've always loved that first line, about a certain slant of light. It's sad and sends a little shiver down my spine. I wrote it down, my first day here, down on the beach – and then my own poem just sort of grew out of it.'

And then, staring joyfully at Miss Welbeck, she realized. 'You believe it was my poem then?'

'Yes, I do, Rebecca.'

All this time Elizabeth Exton had been sitting like some-one turned to stone, except for a trembling of the lips that she was not able to control. As Miss Welbeck turned to her, she burst forth.

'I didn't know it was Rebecca's poem. I had no idea! A holidaymaker gave it to me down on the beach. I thought *she'd* written it. She said I could have it.'

'You took her advice very literally,' said Miss Welbeck in acid tones. 'Did you not recognize the handwriting?'

'It was written in block capitals,' said Elizabeth coldly. 'Of course, if only Rebecca had turned it in for the magazine, I would have known at once.' She turned on Rebecca quite savagely. 'Why didn't you do that?'

'I'd thrown it away – I couldn't remember it!' said Rebecca. She was no longer frightened or shy of the imposing Sixth Former. The mighty had fallen very low. 'Besides, as I'd taken the opening line from a proper poem, it wasn't really my own work.'

'True, true,' said Miss Welbeck. 'Though you could have made an acknowledgement. I was mildly surprised that it carried no acknowledgement when I first saw it. And that reminds me –'

Briskly Miss Welbeck picked up the telephone extension that went directly through to the School Secretary.

'Have any of the magazines been despatched yet, Sarah?' she asked. 'No? Good. Good. Hold them. None is to go out. I want some erratum slips printed. I'll give you details in the morning.' She put the telephone down and glanced at her watch. 'Elizabeth, you will remain with me. We must talk. Rebecca. You, I'm afraid, have completely missed your tea. So, I daresay, has Ishbel Anderson. Miss Morgan had instructions to keep her in her office.'

The Principal picked up the 'phone for the last time and dialled through to Miss Morgan's office at Juniper.

'Madeleine Welbeck here. The matter of the poem is resolved. Rebecca Mason is its author, with a little help from Emily Dickinson. Please tell Ishbel Anderson that I will see her in the morning. In the meantime I would like you to take both girls out to tea at the Vienna Restaurant. Charge it to the school account.'

'Please,' Rebecca blurted out shyly, 'Sue Murdoch hasn't had any tea either. She's Tish – she's Ishbel's best friend and she's been crying buckets.'

'Then she must go too,' said the Principal, with a hint of a smile. 'It may speed her recovery a little.'

She watched as Rebecca rushed out of the study, the last of the daylight catching her fair hair, and thought, 'What an interesting child she is.'

Then she turned to Elizabeth Exton and the disagreeable task ahead. 'Vaunting ambition,' thought Miss Welbeck. She must talk to Elizabeth about that. Some causes you won, and some you lost. Elizabeth, Miss Welbeck now realized, was a lost cause, cast too much in the Exton mould.

*

'Are you going to ring father now?' asked Tish sullenly, as Miss Morgan replaced the telephone receiver. 'What did Miss Welbeck say?'

As she waited for the House Mistress to reply, her mind went over the ground yet again. Why couldn't Miss Morgan have 'phoned her father straight away? Why didn't they just let her go? It was going to come to that in the end. Elizabeth Exton would never own up. Rebecca would stick to her guns, but it was only her word against Elizabeth's, and nobody would believe her. Well, Tish wasn't going to retract a thing. She'd rather leave Trebizon than do that, and that was saying something. It was the best place on earth, for a school.

Poor Rebecca. They weren't going to punish her, just treat her as some sort of nut case. Pack her off to see Dr Carson, that psychologist person, likely as not. Like they had Millicent Dawson when she had gone on that shoplifting spree. Why wasn't Miss Morgan saying anything? She'd put the 'phone down hours ago. Why was she just staring into space with that red tinge creeping up her face?

'Can you get my father to come and fetch me now, please?'

Miss Morgan came to. She spoke in a voice full of emotion.

'Of course not, Ishbel. I've been told to take you and Rebecca out to tea at the Vienna Restaurant.'

'Tea –?'

'That's right. It seems we have misjudged you. Miss Welbeck has seen Rebecca and she is completely satisfied that she is the author of the poem.'

'She *is* –?'

Tish jumped to her feet and danced round and round the

office, flung open the door and danced into the corridor –
and crashed into Rebecca.

'Tish!'

'Rebeck!'

They grabbed hands and twisted round and round outside Miss Morgan's office, until the walls spun. Rebecca felt
delirious with happiness. Was it only dinner break when she
had last seen Tish, and they had looked together at her
poem in the school magazine? It seemed at least a fortnight
ago. So much had happened since then.

'Stop it, you'll be sick,' said Miss Morgan, laughing, all
the tension leaving her.

Rebecca very nearly was sick that evening. Miss Morgan
took her and Tish and Sue down to the town for the most
sumptuous tea at the Vienna Restaurant. They consumed
hot toasted muffins and trifle and jelly and ice-cream
and huge chocolate eclairs stuffed full of fresh dairy
cream.

As if that weren't enough, the three girls rounded off the
day with a celebration at Moffatt's, the school tuck shop,
with the other members of Tish's 'Action Committee',
Margot Lawrence and Sally Elphinstone and Mara
Leonodis.

'Papa will laugh his head off when I tell him the excitement he has given us,' said the Greek girl. 'With the little
duplicating machine, I mean. Who would have thought it
could do so much good!'

'I bet Freddie Exton won't laugh,' said Margot, soberly.

'Do you think he'll ask for his money back?' asked
Rebecca. 'All the money he put into the school magazine?'

'Not likely!' Tish's big laugh was back in place and the
bounce was back in her bobbing curls. 'As if he'd dare.
Besides, he's still got Margaret at the school.' She finished

on a dry tone. 'Who knows, she might want to be Editor one day.'

Elizabeth Exton had already gone: she had caught the seven o'clock train to London. As she watched the lights of Trebizon town twinkling into the distance behind her, she wondered what the future held in store for her. She made a vow. If she ever met up with Tish Anderson again in the big wide world, she would find some way to get her revenge.

The mood in Juniper House that night was one of great jubilation and emotion. In both the Second Year and First Year dormitories the girls could talk of nothing but the great scandal of the day and the way that *The Juniper Journal* had, in the end, emerged with honour. Even those girls who had sided with Elizabeth Exton and authority, conveniently forgot about it or else had the grace to admit that they had been wrong.

Josselyn Vining met Rebecca on the second floor landing, just after she had cleaned her teeth for bed. For the umpteenth time that night, Rebecca found herself being congratulated on her poem.

'Of course, I'm not an expert, but it seems pretty good to me for someone of our age,' said Joss. She added ruefully, 'Wish you were as keen on hockey as you are on writing.'

'But I am,' said Rebecca.

'Then why didn't you come to the trial at the beginning of term?' asked Joss. 'That's what I can't understand.'

'Trial?' said Rebecca. '*Trial?* I thought it was just an ordinary practice game. That was the night I was trying to write something for *The Trebizon*. I mean, I'd never really played hockey before, and Debbie never told me it was a trial. I don't think I'd have believed her if she had!'

'So that was why!' exclaimed Joss, in some anger. 'It was a

trial all right. Judy's marvellous at right wing, but she's got a funny ankle and has to drop out of matches sometimes. I thought you might make a good reserve, especially for Judy. If I ask Miss Willis if you can play at right wing in games tomorrow, would you like that? We would see how you get on.'

'Like it?' said Rebecca. 'Of course, I'd like it!'

At Assembly next morning, Miss Welbeck announced Elizabeth Exton's departure and then hastily passed on to happier news.

'You all should know that the Upper Sixth Form held a special meeting last night and unanimously elected a new Editor for *The Trebizon Journal*. Audrey Maxwell will hold that post for the rest of the school year.'

Loud clapping burst out in the hall.

Audrey's first task in her new post was to go down to the printers and organize the printing of a batch of small gummed slips. The printer was able to run them off the same day.

That evening a large team of volunteers went through every single copy of the Golden Jubilee edition of *The Trebizon Journal* and stuck the gummed slips over Elizabeth Exton's name, at the end of the poem. It now read: *By Rebecca Mason Form II Alpha (with acknowledgements to Emily Dickinson)*. The magazines were now ready to be dispatched.

Rebecca played well in her trial position as right wing in the hockey lesson that afternoon. In due course, it was announced that she had been made a reserve for the school's Under-Fourteen team.

In the second half of the term, Judy Sharp's ankle only let her down once, just before a home match against Caxton High School. In her sole appearance in the school team,

Rebecca acquitted herself well – setting up one goal for Tish, at left inner, and another for Sue, at right.

There was something very pleasing about that, for the three girls were friends and inseparable now. By the end of term, Rebecca's first weeks at Trebizon, when she had had no special friends, were no more than a memory.

Her parents flew back to England for Christmas and met her off the train. They had already read *The Trebizon Journal*, which had been waiting for them at home, from cover to cover.

'I see you had a poem printed, Becky,' said her father proudly, as they drove away from the station. 'I thought it was going to be an essay.'

'It was,' said Rebecca. 'One day I'll tell you all about it.'

'Have you enjoyed your first term?' asked her mother anxiously. 'Have you really enjoyed it?'

'Yes, Mum. I really have.'

She was looking forward to Christmas at home. She was also looking forward to going back to school in January and seeing Tish and Sue, and seeing the winter sea through the bare trees from her dormitory window again.

What a contrast to her feelings when she had set off on the train for her first term at Trebizon! Would the second term be as good as the first?

Rebecca knew that she would have to wait and see.